THE BLOODLINES OF SAHAEL

VOLUME TWO

BOOK FOUR

YORUBAN REMNANTS

BY

DWAYNE ANTHONY MADRY

Copyright © 2025 by Dwayne A. Madry
All rights reserved. This book or any portion thereof
may not be reproduced or used in any manner whatsoever
without the express written permission of the publisher
except for the use of brief quotations in a book review.

Printed in the United States of America

First Printing, 2025

Cover Design by JessHavok

ISBN 978-1-963089-41-7

www.SAHAEL.com

Intoduction into Sahael

Aamira's journey was not merely a tale of epic battles and heroic triumphs; it was also a deeply personal odyssey fraught with obstacles and tribulations that tested her very spirit. As she navigated the complexities of her family relationships, the weight of expectation and the shadows of her past often loomed large, making her quest to thrive in the desert Sandlands of IFF even more challenging. Yet, through it all, Aamira remained resolute. She was determined to rise above the difficulties, driven by the unwavering love for her people and the fierce desire to ensure their survival. In her relentless pursuit, Aamira had become a beacon of hope, saving her people from the brink of despair and guiding them toward a future where they could flourish safely in their harsh environment. The desert, once a place of peril, transformed into a sanctuary under her leadership, as she fostered a sense of community and resilience among her kin. Through tireless research and unwavering dedication, Aamira delved into the ancient wisdom of her ancestors, merging their time-honored teachings with modern insights. Each discovery was a piece of the puzzle, illuminating the path to restoring health and happiness to her people. As she unearthed forgotten remedies and sustainable practices, she laid the groundwork for a thriving society that could withstand the challenges of their surroundings. Her hard work bore fruit as Aamira's initiatives took root, revitalizing the spirit of her community. The gardens flourished, producing nourishing crops that fed both body and soul, while the bonds of kinship grew stronger in the face of adversity. Aamira's vision was becoming a reality—a flourishing haven in the heart of the desert, where her people could find solace, purpose, and a renewed sense of identity. Despite the progress she made, Aamira faced the constant struggle of balancing her personal life with her responsibilities as a leader.

The complexities of family dynamics often tested her resolve, yet she persevered, knowing that her efforts were critical to the future of her people. She drew strength from her struggles, using them as fuel to propel her forward, and reminding herself that every challenge was an opportunity for growth. As she looked toward the horizon, the promise of SAHAEL—the legendary sanctuary of safety and enlightenment—beckoned to her like a distant dream. Aamira understood that the journey to reclaiming their ancestral home was not just about physical relocation; it was about restoring their heritage, their culture, and their connection to the land. With renewed vigor, she sought solutions to guide her people back to this fabled place, weaving together the threads of knowledge, unity, and hope. With each passing day, Aamira became more determined to lead her people to SAHAEL, where they could rediscover their legacy and build a brighter future. Her heart swelled with the belief that together, they could overcome any obstacle, break free from the chains of their past, and emerge as a vibrant community ready to embrace the promise of tomorrow. In this epic chapter of their lives, Aamira stood as a testament to resilience, embodying the spirit of the Yoruban remnants. She was not just a leader; she was a symbol of hope, a fierce protector of her people's dreams, and a catalyst for change. The path ahead would be fraught with challenges, but Aamira was ready to face them, armed with the knowledge of her ancestors and the unwavering love for her kin, as she charted a course toward a new dawn in SAHAEL.

CHAPTER CONTENTS

CHAPTER I   THE NIBIRU WALL   1

CHAPTER II   THE LOST & FOUND   Page 38
                 BLOODLINE

CHAPTER III   A DYAD IN THE   Page 62
                 BLOODLINE

CHAPTER IV   INHERITANCE ISLAND   Page 78

CHAPTER V   THE SIGNS OF THE TIMES   Page 100

CHAPTER I
THE NIBIRU WALL

Aarde, Timbuktu, The Ancient Library

Aamira washed her body from a basin of cold water on the library quarters balcony overlooking Timbuktu. Normally she wouldn't have stood naked in the sun for an entire city to see, but since Timbuktu was completely empty, and the balcony could not be seen from other parts of the twenty-story library, she thought no harm would be done. The city sparkled in the morning light, a beautiful gem of engineering and architecture.

Too bad it had been abandoned now for at least a decade.

As she washed her arms, Aamira reflected on her life up to this point, from the few memories she had of living in the palace before Sahael's destruction, through her youth on the plantation waiting to be sold off for her virtue. Now she had been married for decades to a good man, had four strapping sons, was the queen of IFF, the empress of Neros's Realm, and yet still a refugee from her barren homeland. And here she bathed in broad daylight on a library balcony overlooking what could easily be described as a dead city.

In other words, she still had a lot of work to do.

"If I'd known you would be bathing naked on the balcony, I would have waited to clean myself up," Abioye's voice sounded from behind her.

Aamira turned to see her husband smiling, arms folded over his simple colorful traveling garb. He was handsome, dark skin catching the light of the late morning sun, white teeth shining. His dreadlocks fell to his broad shoulders. Abioye hadn't aged a day since they met almost thirty years ago.

"You know I like to bathe alone," Aamira said coyly.

"A husband can still fantasize, can't he?" Abioye grinned.

"I thought you were going to search the city with the boys for more supplies and fruit from the trees that are still alive," Aamira said.

Abioye nodded. "Yekú, Yomí, Yemí, Yinká and I were about to head out when one of the sailors came up from the kitchens and told me Adewara wants to see us. We'll have to gather supplies later this afternoon."

Laughter bubbled in Aamira's chest. "When was the last time Educator Adewara called for us and it didn't take the entirety of the day?"

"Point taken," Abioye agreed. "Still, we should meet him in the Yoruban Hall on the 15th level as usual. I'll let you get dressed, unless you want me to disrobe and join you."

"There will be plenty of time for that later," Aamira smiled.

"Not if Adewara has his way." He stepped forward and kissed his wife on the cheek. "He'll be blathering on for hours and hours. I'll meet you in the Yoruban Hall with the boys. Don't take too long."

Abioye stepped out, leaving Aamira to get dressed in silence. They had only been in Timbuktu for two days, but she already felt restless. Only five of the nine sailors from Neros's Realm, including Admiral Adbul, had survived the ocean journey and climbed through the caves to reach A.M.I.T. and Timbuktu. Danger would only increase from here, and they could not stop on their journey to redeem Sahael. Hopefully Adewara would share a plan today and not merely more history, though her experience with the Educator meant she understood the likelihood of a straightforward conversation being about as probable as Aamira sprouting angel's wings.

Aamira threw on a silk robe she had found in a closet in their library quarters and made her way down the stairs to the 15th level. She entered the Yoruban Hall with its many bookshelves and green Bear sigils. Adewara stood at the central study table surrounded by scrolls, collections of bound brass plates, and leather maps. Aamira's four sons, Yekú, Yomí, Yemí, and Yinká sat beside their father, looking intuitive and earnest, something that surprised her. Normally her adult children were bored by Adewara's lectures, but it seems that since arriving in Timbuktu, they had gained a greater appreciation for his teachings.

Either that, or they really didn't want to explore the city looking for supplies.

"Aamira," Adewara said, waving his arm for her to join them. His dark afro, with its speckles of gray, caught the morning light like a halo around his head. "I was just telling your family that I've been looking for clues of what to do next. I've continued to search through the white leather books of the Hornans, seeing if I could find any clues. The ship's crew has been working the kitchens under Yekú's tutelage."

"I've actually learned a lot from them about how to prepare dried meals from a ship's storage," Yekú added. "Admiral Abdul is a surprisingly good cook. He practiced as a Bozeman under his first captain and had to learn everything he could about the kitchen and meal preparation. He knows how to make even stale bread taste good with the right spices and a bit of broth. Since much of what we've found here in Timbuktu has been dried grains and fruits, it's been very helpful. I think all of you have enjoyed the meals."

"In any case," Adewara said as if to bring the conversation back to what he had planned, "I have found some information that will help determine how we can get closer to Sahael. I've poured through vast and new knowledge of the Hornan and Roman teachings as you all slept. I've learned that the Romans are all over Aarde and have been stuck in western Aarde without any way to travel east beyond the Nibiru wall."

"Why are they even beyond the Nibiru wall?" Aamira asked. "I thought that's why the wall was built by the ancients in the first place, to separate east from west."

"We kept track of them through NeRu's eye but lost track of them the day Sahael was invaded, and Khartoum Palace was destroyed," Adewara said. "Since then, many things have shifted as Natas has spread his influence. The ancient library here has a full recording of history from across Aarde. Our Educators record their history in secret, allowing us to physically know where nationalities like the Romans are at all times. We can't track them through NeRu's eyes currently. Hopefully when Sahael is restored, we can resume tracking once more."

"All they're doing is roaming?" Aamira questioned. "That's all they did for a century. There has to be more to it than that."

"According to our lessons back in Neros's realm while Yinká was a baby," Yomí said, tapping one of the sets of brass plates, "Roman citizens were dubbed 'Roamers' because once their city fell, they had no leadership and simply roamed through other nations stealing resources."

"The Roamers were ordered to roam Aarde per the command of Egyptus," Adewara explained. "It was Sahael's duty to watch and track their every movement and the role of the Educators to record their entire history."

"Do they even have a home to roam to?" Abioye asked.

Adewara fiddled with the braids in his beard, as if it would help him explain things better. "Yes, Rome and the Trome Lands, but the remnant of the people are forbidden to go and inhabit those areas. If the Roamers were to ever return to their homeland, war would break out; a war Rome could never win. Sooner or later Egyptus and Rome are destined to go to war. It's been prophesied by oracles on both sides of the conflict. This is why they roam day and night, week after week, month after month, and year after year."

"I don't think that's fair at all," Aamira said. "Sooner or later, they're going to have to return home, and we'll have to deal with the fallout of what happens."

Picking up one of the fabric scrolls, Adewara handed it to Aamira. "The books you see here are a past record of their history but don't reveal their locations. The Roamers need to be found first. Only then can we get to Sahael in a timely manner."

"Why?" Yinká asked, face thoughtful as always.

"Lord Commander Natas systematically infiltrated Narsa and took complete control of the island and its people using phylacteries filled with the White Darkness," Adewara explained. "We do know our one and only witan Educator, Ally, made it look like he succumbed to the white darkness. He has d to appear to the witans that he became lost, Ally recorded the entire event of it taking place in Narsa in his Nalace journal." Adewara held up a thick leather-bound book. "I have the record right here."

"Does it say how this White Darkness found its way into

Aarde?" Aamira asked. The White Darkness had been a whispered mystery for years, with the slaves on the plantation talking about how Natas used it to corrupt minds. Aamira doubted any of that, feeling personally that power was the ultimate corruptor, and that Natas offered the weaker nations power in exchange for help destroying Sahael. White Darkness was self-corruption, nothing more.

"I know we've had this conversation before, Empress Aamira," Adewara continued, "But it can't be denied that this White Darkness seems to influence the minds of the people in each of the witan nations. Lord Commander Natas did this to control the entire country and every single Narsan man and woman, young and old. Natas ordered the Narsans to infiltrate The States of 'Or, the 'Arth Nations, The Sovereign Dales, and reluctantly, Triennium Island. Lord Commander Natas enslaved the minds of their leaders, using the White Darkness for his own benefit. Afterwards, Natas indoctrinated the witan nations with his teachings of the Nauthian gospel and creed."

Aamira shook her head. "And that just proves my point. The 'White Darkness' isn't a real thing. It's another one of Natas's tools for giving witans an excuse to give into their darkest impulses. Natas offered them power and they took it. There is no excuse for what the witans have done to our people. I saw the rape and murder on the plantations before the revolts. I will never give witans an excuse or the White Darkness to wash away their culpability in massacre and enslavement. I don't care what this witan Educator Ally wrote. White Darkness was and is his excuse as well, if you ask me."

The family sat silent for a moment, feeling the weight of Aamira's words. Even Adewara, rarely speechless, looked at the table contemplatively.

"In any case," Adewara spoke eventually, "according to

Ally's record, the White Darkness moved through the leaders who had given themselves over completely to their ambition."

"Does this White Darkness affect Black people?" Aamira asked with a fake smile.

"No, it only affects the minds of fragile witans and sellouts," Adewara replied in a confident and steady voice.

"The weak minded can never be trusted no matter what skin color they have," Abioye said.

"What happened once he had all these witans either under his control or convinced of their superiority?" Yomí asked.

"After gaining control of the western powers, Lord Commander Natas now had in his possession the most powerful nation on the other side of the Nibiru wall," Adewara answered. "The other nations quickly signed his treaty to be part of the invasion force, and they would provide resources for Narsa."

"A treaty? That's wild," Yemí said, shaking his head.

"The Supremacy Pact," Adewara confirmed. "A group of witan nations whose only goal was to spread Lord Commander Natas's supremacy all over Western Aarde. After building up their economies, Natas held a council in which he invited all the leaders of the 'Arth Nations, the States of 'Or, Triennium, the Dales, the T.I.M. nations and Narsa to determine how they would find a way into Eastern Aarde beyond the Nibiru wall."

"This had to have taken a lot of time," Abioye said. "I mean, we know that the wall was not easily avoided. Plus, some of the national powers you're talking about haven't been nations themselves since before the fall of Sahael. How long are we talking about here?"

"After 150 years, Lord Commander Natas was able to gain control of the Nibiru wall," Adewara continued. "Natas sent one of his Triennium commanders to secure the ancient barrier. In a few weeks, the Triennium Commander was able to gain control of both the Nibiru wall and castle. Since then, according to these records, the Nibiru wall in that sector of Aarde has been operated by the Rysallians. They now determine who gains access into Eastern and Western Aarde."

Yinká stood, visibly angry at the news Adewara was sharing. "Perhaps it would have been better if the wall was simply destroyed by Natas. That wall has brought the people of Western Aarde nothing but angst and torment."

"I agree," Aamira said. "Living in the Vannadale Colony, the Nibiru wall was a topic of frustration for everyone."

"I don't get it," Yekú said. "I know I was always more interested in learning recipes than in history, but the Nibiru Wall doesn't sound as important as all of you are making it out to be. Why should we care that Natas has control of it?"

"The Nibiru wall is made out of Orichalcum," Adewara answered. "It is indestructible. Natas took control of the Nibiru wall when he learned it couldn't be destroyed. With the wall under Narsan control, this enabled the next phase of Natas's plan involving the Trinity to begin. With control of the wall, Lord Natas was able to invade Eastern Aarde a second time after the conference in Nycea."

Yekú looked around the room. "I'm drawing a blank here. What is the Conference in Nycea?"

"Really?" Yinká said, shaking his head. "Your little brother is going to have to school you on our people's history?"

"Yekú always paid more attention to the girls in the kitchens than he did his studies," Yomí laughed.

"Lord Commander Natas ordered the Narsans to capture several Alkebulans before the council was held in Nycea in Eastern

Aarde," Yinká explained. "The enslaved Alkebulans were displayed in front of those in attendance. The people of what was known as the Great-8 nations were in awe with the size of the women and the men and their physiques. They were dressed in their fine clothing as they were taken away like slaves; the first to be enslaved, in truth."

"Well said, High King Yinká," Adewara smiled. "It's good to know not all of my lessons fell on deaf ears."

"I hope that title doesn't stick," Yemí whispered to his fellow triplets.

"Yeah, Adewara," Yomí said. "We know our brother is meant to be High King in Sahael, but we know Yinká is going to get a big head with you calling him that all the time."

"I will do my best to refrain, Prince Yomí," Adewara smiled.

"Can we get back to the first enslavement, please?" Abioye urged. "What new details have you learned, Adewara?"

"Quite a bit over the last 24 hours, to be honest," Adewara said. "According to the record of Educator Quintus from the far lands, Lord Commander Natas used lies and deception and told the G-8 that the Blacks in Alkebulan possess a land with unlimited resources. Natas also convinced the eight nations that Blacks in Alkebulan were stupid, mindless, and barbaric, in need of saving. Taking the resources from them would be a blessing to all, since obviously the Sahaelians were too degenerate to use them properly. Natas said that their Black souls were damned, convincing the G-8 it needed to bring the Nauthian gospel to the Black people. He then convinced the G-8 to go along with what he wanted them to do. It was determined that after four months, four weeks, and four days of Conferences and meetings that Lord Commander Natas and the Trinity would divide up the land into thirds along with its resources."

"Of course they would," Yomí said, stretching his neck. "All witans want to do is take from everyone else."

Adewara sat back, placing his hands behind his head. "It may seem that way, but ignorance is the fastest way to suffering and death. I myself learned that truth just this morning. I feel quite humble at this moment."

"What do you mean?" Aamira asked. Adewara was not one for self-deprecation. If he had been humbled by something, she wanted to know what.

"I have kept our path pointed as straight toward Sahael as possible under the circumstances," Adewara replied. His face suddenly looked sad, as if some great mistake had been made. "Reading the journals pointed me toward a record I have read many times before, but for some reason I overlooked one important thing regarding the redemption of Sahael."

"And what is that?" Abioye questioned.

A deep breath filled Adewara's lungs. He put his hands back on the table and leaned forward. "All of us have been tainted by Natas and the actions of our witan brothers. All of us have embraced hate, just as they have. I say to myself that I don't hate all witans, and yet, when I see one, I have a desire to harm them. Am I alone in this?"

Everyone looked at the table. Abioye fiddled with one of the maps as if it was the most interesting thing in the world.

"That's what I thought," Adewara said. "Still, there is one passage I've read over and over during my studies these past decades, but it has never registered until now. *And the blood of the Rysallians will feed Sahael in her redemption, brought by the Yoruban bloodline. The Sentinel Islands shall be united into one landmass as the six bloodlines shed blood together on the altar of sacrifice. And hate will be washed away, for brother will stand with brother, and old ties will be renewed; for in that day, Sahael will bask in joy as the mists flee and the Yoruban and Rysallian cleans the land united.*"'"

"What does that mean?" Yinká asked.

"It means that in order for your Yoruban bloodline to perform its duty in the reclaiming of Sahael, at least one representative of the Rysallian bloodline must be present with you."

"A witan?" Yomí spat. "Why would the very people who joined Natas to wipe us out and enslave us ever be allowed to set foot in Sahael, let alone help us save her?"

Aamira had to admit; she shared her son's frustration. Witans had not shown her or her people mercy in any way. Why would they be required to save Sahael?

Adewara continued, answering the questions both spoken and unspoken. "Not all witans are evil or controlled or influenced. Many of them are known to have fought against Natas, and I would assume many of them still do. Evil is not confined to one skin color; nor is bravery and sacrifice. I have been blind to this fact, and because of it, I would have led us to Sahael on a mission we never could have achieved. We must have a Rysallian with us if Sahael is to be redeemed."

No one spoke. No one breathed. Such a revelation was completely unexpected. Aamira didn't know what to think.

"This doesn't make sense," Abioye said after a few moments. "The witan bloodline is the reason Sahael, Alkebulan, and the realms were enslaved in the first place. Every nation in Alkebulan has been at war with witans in the west for over 500 years. According to the Nairobi Laws, which my father, and you yourself Adewara, made me read many times as a youth, if a witan is brought to Sahael, then all of what you're working to achieve will have been for nothing. The Signs of the Times will no longer protect the chosen bloodlines of Sahael. Am I wrong?"

Eyes shifting back and forth as if in furious thought, Adewara rubbed his upper lip. "You are not wrong. This is a contradiction to be sure. But it's clear from these passages that Rysallian blood is needed if Sahael is to be reclaimed."

Just then, Admiral Abdul entered the library holding a platter of three soup bowls. His gray dreadlocks and beard were tied into braids to keep them out of the food. A pleasant aroma of rosemary and basil wafted from the soups, making Aamira more than conscious of her hunger.

"I apologize for the intrusion on your discussion, my empress and emperor," Abdul said with a polite bow, "but with Yekú's culinary help since we left Neros's Realm, I have crafted a rather delicious soup that you should have for your mid-day meal."

Aamira stood and motioned for the admiral to bring the soup over. "Thank you, Admiral. You are keeping us well fed."

"Why are there only three bowls?" Yekú asked, face scrunched in disappointment.

Abdul smiled. "I was told you young men would be out scouting the city for fresh supplies."

"And you can make your own soup later," Abioye grinned as he grabbed one of the bowls and drank deeply of the broth.

Aamira sat back and folded her arms. The idea of a Rysallian needing to accompany them to Sahael continued to vex her mind. "What do you know of the Trinity, Admiral Abdul? And of the Rysallian bloodline? As a sailor, you must have interacted with other races during your voyages. I'd be interested to hear your perspective on these people."

Handing Aamira one of the soup bowls, and Adewara the last of the three, Admiral Abdul rubbed his beard. "The Trinity were the remnants of the Rysallians and other witan bloodlines. Originally the Rysallians were close friends if not apart of the bloodlines of Sahael, seen as brothers and comrades of the Ancient Order for many centuries. It is said that pure-blooded Rysallians still live and fight against Natas on the other side of the Nibiru Wall."

"Your information is dated," Yomí said. "You were all but frozen in time for 50 years. Since then, all witans have become corrupted."

"Perhaps," Abdul nodded. "Though I doubt what you say is fully true. Corruption is a choice; a choice not all people will make. I would bet there are far more witans than you imagine fighting for the freedom of their families and those of the Sahaelian remnants as well."

"Well said, Admiral," Adewara said as he sipped his soup. "Your knowledge is confirmed in what I've been able to read since we arrived here in Timbuktu."

"Sailing the oceans of Aarde has given me a lot to ponder over the decades," Abdul continued. "Even though we in Neros's Realm were trapped in the time loop for so long, as Yomí said, I find that when I sailed before the fall of Sahael, I saw people far more diverse and complicated than what we read in histories. I understand a great many of our people live enslaved, but I can't help but remember the witans I worked and sailed with who were good people."

"Well, they're not anymore," Yemí interrupted. "I've never met a witan who did anything but try to kill me."

"And how many witans have you met?" Abdul asked, a slight smile pulling at his lips.

Yemí shrugged and grunted.

"Exactly," Admiral Abdul replied. "Life is far more complicated than you imagine, and I am willing to bet there are still many witans who fight against Natas with as much ferocity as you do. If all you do is look for enemies, allies will be hard to find."

Aamira blinked at the admiral's words. Had she been looking for enemies wherever they went? She certainly hadn't been looking for allies.

"How were the Trinity able to gain control of Alkebulan?" Yomí inquired, returning to their original subject. "I just want to remind everyone that it was in fact the Trinity, the witan bloodlines, that conquered our people."

Adewara breathed deeply. "You speak of control of Alkebulan, but the Trinity never gained that control. Natas's armies attacked, the kings and queens were slaughtered, the princesses, including your mother, escaped, and Sahael and the great lands were thus cursed and became uninhabitable to life. The air is poisoned, the water polluted, and all animal life dead."

"All of this for what? Love, you claim?" Aamira spat as a gust of wind blew in from the open balcony. "Natas knows nothing of love. He only knows selfishness. He did all of this just to prove his plan is better than his own parent's plan for all the inhabitants of Aarde."

Yinká stood from the table and leaned over the maps. "What are Natas's weaknesses? We've talked about history and witans plenty, but eventually we're going to have to face Natas head on. What does that look like? What are our advantages and disadvantages?"

Closing a stack of brass plated records, Adewara reached over and rolled up the map. "Lord Commander Natas has a full recollection of what happened during the civil war in Katunkumene and before. That means he never received a veil like all other spirits possessing a body. Therefore, he remembers everything."

"What does that mean?" Yekú asked, face suddenly concerned.

"It means he has thousands of years of experience," Aamira replied. "Experience in war, experience in history, experience in individual combat."

"Natas has seen so much of human interaction," Adewara continued, "that there are very few ways to surprise him. He sees the pattern of interaction before we realize we've even decided on what action to take. In short, he's seen everything before. I wasn't there, of course, but it was reported by Natas's commanders after the fall of Sahael that he defeated the four kings easily. The four kings were the greatest warriors in all Aarde. That is not an exaggeration. Natas has abilities like yours to conjure weapons, he can skin-change and make himself look like other people and races. He is you, High King Yinká---"

"Here we go again," Yomí smiled, shaking his head.

"---He is like *all* of you," Adewara said, looking at all four princes, "only amplified a thousand-fold. When men like me show reverence to Lord Commander Natas, it is not because we respect and follow him, but rather we understand his danger and respect the fact that underestimating him led to the destruction of the greatest civilization Aarde has ever known."

"So, how do we defeat him?" Yemí asked.

"We redeem Sahael, and then go from there," Adewara said.

For a moment, silence fell, save for the wind blowing from the balcony and rustling the documents on the table. Aamira had met Natas and felt his power firsthand. Still, having Adewara lay things out so starkly filled her with dread. Educators like Adewara loved to pontificate and make things as complicated as possible. To have him speak so succinctly spoke volumes about the man's feelings about, and fear of, Natas.

"I'm hungry," Yinká said, breaking the tension. "And the fact that you are all eating doesn't make it better."

Adewara smiled. "Let's take a break and return later in the day. There is still much to discuss."

"No need," Abioye said, standing and stretching his back. "The boys can go. We had plans to search the city for extra supplies, and they can do that while Aamira and I stay behind. We'll update them if there's more that needs to be discussed amongst us."

"And we can eat!" Yekú grinned.

The boys left the Yoruban library, happy to be escaping more lessons in favor of exploration. Admiral Abdul also left Aamira, Abioye, and Adewara to their discussion, promising dinner would be every bit as delicious as the soup. Aamira finally took her first bite of soup, instantly overcome by the aroma and powerful spices. The admiral truly knew his way around the kitchens. They ate in silence for a bit until Aamira couldn't hold her thoughts inside any longer.

"I'm just going to say it," Aamira blurted. "We need to get to the Nibiru wall as quickly as we can. It's clear that the Nibiru are no longer operating or living on the Nibiru wall. If we need a member of the Rysallian bloodline in order to free Sahael, that is the best place to find one. That is where they last had a stronghold, and that is where the remnant is said to still live. Am I wrong?"

"You are not wrong, my empress," Adewara said.

"How do you expect us to get there, dear?" Abioye asked

between sips of soup.

"The Nabta gates are activated," Aamira replied.

"They are," Adewara said. "Yesterday I climbed to the top floor where the gate resides and examined all the stones. The Nairohenge gates sit in the center of the Royal Library's top floor. Eight of the nineteen are operational with sapphire and emerald energy emanating above them. The Sigils of the Orishan Dragon and now the Yoruban short haired Bear symbols are lit up. When Oadira was here sometime in the past month or two, her group initiated the sequence and activated the gate."

"There we go," Aamira said.

Adewara calmly lifted his soup bowl and drank what remained. "But we have no Navigators or Medjay Gate Guardians to direct us and guide us anywhere. The Nairohenge gates are active but using them will put us somewhere lost forever without the proper guides. It's not worth the risk. The Life Energy from Neros's realm is now slowly pushing itself into and through the continents in Eastern Aarde."

"Then we look for another solution," Aamira said.

"What about the boat given to us by Sariah and Oxossi, the new stewards in Neros's realm?" Abioye asked. "It got us this far. We'd have to climb back down through the giant tree growth, but the boat is still seaworthy."

"Take the ship all the way to the Nibiru wall then?" Adewara asked.

"Yes, if it helps us get closer to Sahael," Aamira said.

"Indeed," Abioye agreed.

"The boat we arrived on is too small to make the trip. We were never on the open sea during our journey here. We always sailed within sight of land. Such is the requirement of a ship that size."

Aamira put down her spoon. "I understand that, Adewara, but there are hundreds of ships below the city of Timbuktu on the other side of the docks. We saw them there. Some of them were quite large. I think we should talk to the sailors and see if any of the larger ships are sailable and if we have enough people to crew them."

"Do we have to climb down the weird multi-tree plant in the caverns again?" Abioye asked. "Perhaps we can get back to the docks from here somewhere in the city. We lost three sailors during that climb. We can't afford anyone else falling to their deaths, especially since the sailors are the only ones who have the skill to do what we're talking about. The boys and I learned a lot during the voyage, but Neros's crew are the only asset we have."

"The Nairohenge gates and adjacent buildings are linked to the docks," Adewara answered. "I saw it on the city maps yesterday and confirmed it when I checked on the gates themselves. There are access tunnels that lead directly back to the docks if the Nairohenge gates were to ever become inoperable. My order was able to use the Nairohenge to make it somewhere safe after the fall of Sahael when the Nabtahenge gates retracted into the ground in Sahael."

"We should probably go down and see if any ships are usable," Abioye said.

Adewara stood and motioned toward the door. "Follow me."

Aamira and Abioye followed Adewara to the center of the library where the Nairohenge Gates were located. They found the ancient Kemetic symbol of the Marula Tree on the ground with a circular cover that led beneath the surface. Adewara removed the circular cover revealing a set of stone steps descending into darkness.

"You may want to activate your tattoos, so we have some light," Adewara said.

The walls glowed green against Aamira and Abioye's illuminated tattoos. The staircase descended seemingly forever, which made sense after the length of their initial climb into the city. After twenty minutes, the trio stepped onto caves that housed the docks. A shaft of light shot down from openings in the rocks above, illuminating hundreds of ships, all seemingly built with the skill of the ancients.

"One of these ought to work," Abioye smiled.

Adewara turned to face his emperor and empress. "So, are we choosing to do this? It will take days to stock whichever ship we select, and at least two months to sail to the wall. From there, we have no idea what we are going to face."

"How is that any different than anything we do?" Aamira asked.

"Point taken, empress," Adewara nodded.

Abioye pointed to the largest ship on the docks, a vessel with fine carvings and tall masts. It truly looked regal.

"I'm choosing that one," he said.

"Why that one?" Aamira asked.

"First off, it's huge. I mean, it has a dozen cannons on each side. Second, who in their right mind would attack that ship? It looks like it could carry a hundred warriors."

A smile filled Adewara's face. "That is not a bad strategy. Natas loves to intimidate people. Maybe we should take a page out of that book and intimidate the pirates and Narsans we're likely to face."

"And if anyone is foolish enough to try and board us," Aamira said, "we'll go down fighting and take a few hundred of them with us!"

With only 13 people crewing the ship, every day of sailing required each person to perform multiple jobs. Admiral Abdul barked orders and kept them on-task. Aamira had gotten quite good at tying knots and raising sails. Even with the workload, the trip was successful, and far less stressful than when they had left Neros's Realm for Timbuktu. Several times Narsan ships had sailed alongside the massive vessel and shouted for them to be boarded in the name of Natas, but Aamira and Abioye would simply stand on the prow and look down on them silently until the enemy sailors tucked their proverbial tails between their legs and navigated away.

"I'm still surprised no one has tried to attack us along the shipping lanes," Yekú said one evening as he brought dinner up for everyone on the top deck.

"The Narsan's have never seen a ship quite like this one," Admiral Abdul explained as he set plates on the table, wind blowing through his gray dreadlocks. "In truth, I've never seen a ship quite like this one. It harkens back to the legends of Sahael from before most people were born. In the Narsan minds I'm sure they're imagining an army of Sahaelian warriors hidden below deck. And the fact that your parents have never spoken back when they've shouted orders only helps to reinforce the mystique."

"Do you really think we'll find a Rysallian witan that doesn't hate our skin somewhere along the wall?" Yemí asked. "I don't want to say this trip is going to be for nothing, but the chances of finding someone on our side is going to be slim."

"Perhaps," the admiral agreed. "But dungeons are always filled with dissenters and rebels. We need look no further than the chains of oppression to find someone who would fight with us."

Yomí grabbed a piece of bread and sat down. "How many more days until we reach the wall, do you think, Admiral?"

"I can't be certain, but within the week, I would guess."

Only two days later, Adewara woke the Royal Family early in the morning and ushered them to the top deck. Mists rose from the ocean, but a towering shadow could be seen in the distance, catching the pale light of dawn.

"Behold, the glory of the ancients. The Nibiru Wall."

Aamira gazed at the object in the pale morning light. It looked like a black line stretching along the horizon. As they approached over the next hour, the object became more impressive. Several hundred feet tall at least, the wall lined the shore and in places allowed the ocean itself to smash against its expanse.

"It looks like it stretches for hundreds of miles going east and west forever," Abioye breathed.

"The Nibiru wall is a masterpiece of exquisite engineering," Adewara said as ocean spray hit their faces. "As you can see, the wall is dark gray orichalcum, with square patterns throughout. As we get closer, you'll see the sigils of the twelve bloodlines: the Orishans, Yorubans, Hausans, Demirrians, Educators, Egyptians, Hornans, and Sahaelians. Back when the wall was fully maintained and magic flowed through the orichalcum, the symbols would glow at night and fires were lit across the top parapets helping ships in the distance avoid crashing into the wall and being destroyed."

"The Nibiru must have been an incredible people to have built something so massive," Aamira said.

Adewara smiled. "Indeed, they were. The Nibiru wall can withstand anything; quakes, tsunamis, typhoons, hurricanes, and sinkholes. It can take and absorb any damage. It is the largest concentration of Orichalcum anywhere on Aarde and took a century to build."

Soon the ship drew into the current that ran along the wall, giving the sailors and the royal family an up-close view. They drew within a few hundred feet. The sun had risen, shining on carvings and symbols, some of which were 100 feet tall.

Adewara pointed at a series of symbols written in a language Aamira didn't recognize.

"We're approaching Goree Castle according to the writing here," he said. "Goree Castle is one of the entry points to western Aarde. Let's stay in this current and learn what we can from the castle. It may be a good place to find any Rysallians that may still fight against Natas."

Admiral Abdul snapped his fingers and pointed at the two closest sailors. "Be ready, men! We know the castle and wall are occupied by enemy forces. Do nothing to draw attention. Be about your work and keep a keen ear for any commands."

"Yes, Admiral!"

As they drew closer, other ships filtered into the current as well. Most of them appeared to be trading vessels, but some were Narsan war ships as well.

Adewara took out his looking glass to get a better view. "I see Narsan guards and a small crew operating the wall. We need to be careful and move quietly."

Goree Castle suddenly came into view, towering in the

center of the Nibiru wall. The castle itself matched the wall, being made of gray orichalcum. Turrets reached high above the wall, making the castle appear far larger than anything Aamira had seen before. A double-sided drawbridge opened like a great mouth on the water allowing ships to pass through to the other side of Aarde. Six ships were already in the queue waiting to be allowed to the western side. The Timbuktu ship floated into line and the sailors dropped the sails so the current itself would push them slowly through.

Two ships passed to Western Aarde over the next hour, shrinking the line to four vessels. The closer they drew to the castle's cave-like mouth, the more people Aamira saw running along the top of the wall. Soldiers seemed to be boarding each ship before it was allowed to continue its journey.

"We'll need to exit the ship," Adewara warned.

"What's going on?" Aamira asked.

"They're going to inspect the transport. It's their job to examine every vessel passing into Western or Eastern Aarde. Goree is the location the Narsans used to force Alkebulan slaves through the door of no return. The Narsans transported over 15 million Alkebulans through that cursed passage. Once through the Nibiru gates, they were enslaved until the end of their natural lives. Goree Castle has the best tactical advantage for hundreds of miles."

"What do we do?" Yekú asked as he looped rope on his arm and tossed it on a pile.

"We need to find a way to pass through inspection without causing a distraction," Adewara whispered. "More ships from the west and east are approaching. They're going to need to be searched as well. After talking with the admiral, I agree that the castle is our best place to find someone of the Rysallian bloodline that is on our side of this conflict. We need to search the dungeons first. That means we'll need a way inside."

As they drew under the shadow of the carved tunnel, several ships passed coming from Western Aarde carrying crates filled with wild animals and birds. Soon the Timbuktu vessel became second in line. The Royal family watched as the ship directly in front of them was boarded and their cargo inspected. Soldiers ran onto the ship as people were led from the lower decks.

"Are you seeing this," Yemí hissed. "Those are our people, and they're in chains.

Indeed, the cargo of the adjacent ship seemed to indeed be enslaved Alkebulan women in obsidian chains.

"We need to do something now!" Aamira said, grabbing the wooden railing in front of her.

"Don't do anything," Adewara warned, grabbing Aamira by the arm. "Those obsidian chains are indestructible and are made to constrict and control. If we try to free them, they'll be killed instantly. And we'll be drawing undo attention to ourselves, which is not what we want."

Flashbacks filled Aamira's mind suddenly of seeing trafficked women enslaved and in chains on the deck of a ship. She was a little girl on the boat her mother had put her on. Her cousins were there with her, terrified and alone.

Sweat started dripping from Aamira's face and burned her eyes. Her heart pounded against her ribcage, forcing her to take deep breaths.

"Are you okay?" Abioye asked, locking his eyes on hers.

"Yeah, just memories from my childhood," Aamira said.

"We need to get off this ship and into that castle," Adewara informed. "The farther we get into the tunnel, the darker it gets.

Use your dark vision to find any entry points."

"What about Abdul and the sailors?" Yinká asked.

"We have forged the proper papers," Admiral Abdul said. "We raided the docks when we stopped at Dorth. We found all the shipping documents we would need for passing through checkpoints. Qasim has always been a skilled forger. We're lucky to have him on our crew. The ship should pass through, and we can dock on the eastern side. Find us there."

"Can you dock and run a ship this size with so few people?" Aamira asked. "Surely it will draw attention when the Narsans see so few of you."

"Let us worry about that, my empress," Abdul said, touching Aamira's arm. "Trust in Ishtar and Obatala. Trust in the redemption of Sahael. We all need to move quickly. It will be our turn for inspection in a matter of minutes. It will be best to flee the ship while we're moving."

Adewara pointed to the stone walls and arched ceiling above. "I see a water vent over there."

"A water vent you say?" Aamira asked. She saw an iron grate about halfway up the arching wall, 100 feet above the water below.

"Yes, these vents were placed to prevent the tunnel from flooding during storm surges," Adewara said. "We can use them to get inside. Everyone from the royal family should get ready to jump across. We need to make sure no one is nearby. There are small ledges in places as you can see. They're only a few inches wide, but you should be able to jump from the ship and hold there until I open the vent."

Adewara looked around as if to verify no soldiers or Narsans were near the ship as it continued moving toward the checkpoint. He then leaped twenty feet over the water, grabbing the seams between the mortared stones and climbing to the vent. He grabbed the iron bars and dangled over the water in the dark tunnel. Aamira, her husband and sons, followed suit, landing on a small ledge not far from the vent. Adewara pulled furiously on the grate, long braids cascading over his shoulder toward the water. He grunted until the mortar broke free and Adewara pushed the grate inside the dark vent. With a nod to the royal family huddled on the ledge, Adewara climbed into the hole.

"Our turn," Abioye said. He jumped from the ledge and scaled the stone wall like a spider. Aamira went next, following the same line as her husband. The stones were moist from the ocean air, but she found enough purchase with her fingers to make it to the vent. Pulling herself up inside, Aamira instantly smelled sewage and human waste. She shimmied her way up, seeing the vent open into a small space above where Adewara and Abioye waited. Very little light filtered up the ventilation shaft. Even with her dark vision, details were sparse.

"It smells like feces up here," Abioye said, waving his hand in front of his nose.

"These vents must be linked to the Nibiru sewers," Adewara replied.

The boys quickly made their way up the shaft to the open area. Everyone complained of the smell.

Adewara pointed behind them, deeper into the ventilation system. "The vent goes back down over here, I'm assuming, to the sewers. That will be the perfect place to enter the dungeons. I know it's not pleasant, but we need to head that way."

Yinká started dry heaving. "Do we really need to do this?"

Adewara replied by making his way to the far end of the tunnel and dropping down the shaft. Everyone else followed.

Aamira landed in complete darkness, splashing into a

chunky liquid that made her want to vomit.

"What the hell?" Yekú swore. "This smells worse than a sweaty cow's ass!"

"I don't want to know what this is!" shouted Yemí.

"It feels like we're standing waist-deep in beef stew," Yomí added.

"It doesn't smell like beef stew!" Yinká said.

"We need to get out of here," Aamira choked. "My throat is hurting, and everyone is going to get sick."

Suddenly the sound of fingernails scratching on stone above drew their attention from the horrid smell.

"Did you all hear that?" Adewara said.

Aamira looked up into the darkness, seeing only the barest of shapes in what little light came in through the shaft. Then she saw several sets of eyes reflecting in the gloom. Each creature appeared to have three eyes, though it was hard to tell even with her dark vision activated.

"Be on your guard everyone! I just saw something jumping from a web," Abioye said.

Something hissed, followed by a loud hooting sound."

"They're spider monkeys," Adewara whispered.

"I don't want to know what a spider monkey is," Yekú said.

"Knowledge is power," Adewara replied. "They're nine-legged creatures that eat the feces in these tanks. Spider monkeys are about the size of regular monkeys. They're hairy, with fangs, three eyes, and are great swimmers."

"And they eat poop," Abioye said.

"They're not dangerous," Adewara explained. "They keep

Nibiru's septic tank clean at all times, preventing the mutated sewer spiders from escaping and creating nests. The spider monkeys will not harm us; let's just get to the surface as quickly as possible."

Adewara and the Royal Family moved through the septic tank slowly. The sewage flowed through a tunnel where light poked through a grate overhead.

"Reach up and see if we can open that cover," Aamira said. Yomí immediately jumped up and grabbed hold of the grate, but it was rusted shut.

"It's no use," Yomí said, dropping back down into the sewage. "The thing's rusted tight."

"There's an ancient Kemetic symbol on this septic cover," Adewara said. Aamira looked closer and indeed saw a carving of the Eye of Horus next to an inscription.

"Make eye contact with it," Adewara said.

"What do you mean?" Aamira asked.

"This castle was built by the ancients. These sewers would have been cleaned by the original Kemite bloodline. Magic and science are everywhere. Place your eye close to the symbol. It may open for us as it would have our great forefathers."

Aamira leaped up and grabbed the grate, pulling her eye close to the symbol. The carving glowed green and the sewer cover opened.

"Let me go first, Mother," Yekú said. "I can see what is up there."

"I'm fine son," Aamira said as she dangled from the now open grate. "I don't need protecting, but I appreciate the gesture."

Aamira pulled herself slowly out of the sewer. She stood in a stone corridor that ran at least 100 yards in a straight course.

Openings in the ceiling let in light. Several side hallways shot off to the left and right both in front and behind her. Water dripped somewhere in the distance, as did the splashing of ocean waves.

The others exited the drain, shaking off what they could of the human waste.

"We need to get cleaned off right now," Abioye warned. "If any of this sewage gets in our systems, we're likely to get incredibly sick, or worse."

"Where are we?" Yinká asked.

"Somewhere inside Goree Castle," Adewara said. "Let's check for access to the water if we can. If we're able to avoid being seen by the guards, they'll definitely smell us."

Searching the corridor, Aamira found an open staircase leading to an inlet of ocean water that seemed to be a washing station for clothing. Tall walls stretched up ten stories, blocking the washing area from view.

"This is perfect," Aamira said. "I don't see any soap anywhere but let's get cleaned up as best we can. And fast."

After a few minutes of swimming in the salty water, the royal family exited smelling much better, but still far from clean.

"At least now we won't be announcing our presence quite so boldly," Yomí joked.

"What's the plan?" Yemí asked as they looked to make sure no soldiers had entered the hallway.

"We explore quietly," Adewara said. "We need to get our bearings and see if we can find any people in the dungeons, or anywhere really, of the Rysallian bloodline. The dungeons would be best though, since that means they've likely been fighting against the Narsans and would be amenable to our cause."

Sneaking around, the royal family discovered several

chambers and hallways that snaked through the castle. While they saw plenty of guards on the outer walls from windows they passed, few soldiers moved around inside the castle itself. Only twice did they need to hide in order to avoid detection. Occasionally they would come on a pile of human bones or the remains of someone long dead, slaughtered on the stairs or in a hallway.

"It's clear the Narsans invaded the castle and killed as many people as they could," Abioye said as they stepped over a desiccated corpse.

"And then refused to clean up after themselves," Yekú said.

"The Narsans killed the Nibirans in the castle rather than enslave them," Adewara said.

As they moved closer to the castle's center, they discovered a spacious ballroom with what looked like Nairohenge stones sunk into the floor. Kemetic symbols lined the circular walls, carved into the dark rock, while large mirrors hung every few feet, giving the feel of eternity as they reflected against each other.

"Is this a gate?" Aamira whispered as they entered the chamber.

"It looks like it, yes," Adewara confirmed. "What you all see are Nairohenge Gates, the same Nairohenge Gates you saw in Neros's realm, and in the ancient library they were built by the Nibiru. The Nibiru are known as the great gate builders. This must have been where the Imperator of the Nibiru could travel back to Sahael. The Nibiru, the Alkebulans, and the Sahaelians were all educated in Timbuktu, along with the four watcher realms. They all agreed to teach and share knowledge. This was done to ensure these powerful Black nations were all on the same page with their support, fealty, and expectations of one another, by establishing balance throughout Aarde."

"What happened to the Nibiru people that controlled these

gates?" Aamira asked as a chill ran up her spine. Everything about this castle made her uncomfortable. The mirrors in particular gave her pause, as she could see every angle of the room at once, along with a dozen reflections of herself.

"When Sahael was invaded and Khartoum palace was destroyed, these gates retracted into the ground just as they did everywhere else. Without access to escape, the people here were slaughtered by their enemies." Adewara paused and looked up at the tall ceiling. "The Nibiru wall is a shell of what it used to be, as is this castle. The Nibiru were too dangerous to leave alive due to the knowledge that they possessed. The ability to build Nairohenge Gates all over Aarde is why they were killed by Lord Commander Natas."

Aamira walked up to one of the mirrors, seeing her tired reflection staring back at her. Dust covered the surface. She wiped at the dust, touching the smooth glasslike surface.

A ray of light burst from the mirror at her touch, shining brightly on Aamira's throat. Images of her taking her mother's life when she was a little girl filled her mind. Thoughts she had pushed away became bright. Every detail, from the feeling of the blade cutting flesh, to the warmth of her mother's blood, amplified in her mind's eye. What had she been forced to do as so young a child? Why had the gods allowed it? Why had her mother forced it on her?

Aamira fell backwards onto the ground gasping and holding her throat as if it had been cut. She coughed and gagged for a moment before regaining her senses. The mirror continued to glow.

"What was that?" Abioye asked as he rushed to her side.

"It was a recollection of pain I caused someone I loved who gave their life for mine," Aamira coughed.

"What are these mirrors," Abioye asked.

"We can discuss that some other time," Adewara said.

Yekú shook his head and stepped closer to Adewara. "If you have information, you better give it to us now. The mirror is still glowing. What is this, some sort of curse?"

The light from the mirror drew toward the center into a single shaft of light. The beam hit the stone on the far wall between two other mirrors.

"Check it out," Abioye nodded toward his sons.

The princes ran over and found that the stone was actually on hinges and could be opened like a cabinet. Inside was a large leather book.

"It's a book," Yemí shouted. "It has an Educator symbol on it."

Aamira stood and looked at Adewara as the Educator examined the book. The sigil of the hooded face and the external eyes stared back. The light from the mirror lessened and began moving from one mirror to the next like a hand on a clock. Every few seconds the light would shift to the next mirror, changing the shadows in the chamber.

"This book is for Educators?" Aamira asked.

"It is for the people of the bloodlines," he replied. "The Educators are in fact part of the bloodlines."

"You are a part of the six sacred bloodlines?" Aamira questioned. "Why haven't you told us until now? We thought Educators were merely instructors, not royals of the sacred houses."

Adewara nodded and caressed the symbol on the book with his thumb. "Educators are instructors plucked from all houses. I am indeed from the lost bloodlines though. I was sent by Solomon, who found out where my people had been in exile for hundreds of years. We've been hunted by the Narsans since the fall of Sahael. The Narsans knew that if they found our order, it would disrupt Ishtar and Obatala's plan from ever taking root in Aarde. The book you have found is one of the sacred records of hidden knowledge. It explains everything about our order."

"So, where are your people then?" Abioye asked.

"The land of Inheritance," Adewara said. "Lord Commander Natas chose to avoid the Inheritance, knowing he couldn't detect life there amidst the volcanic activity. Natas thinks Inheritance is devoid of anything remotely alive. Its surface is covered in black ash with soot everywhere."

"But your people were able to survive," Aamira said.

"Yes. We sought refuge below the surface of Inheritance."

"What are you Educators to the bloodlines of Sahael?" Yinká asked.

"We are the keepers of knowledge and all secrets within Aarde. We know all, keep all, and remember all that is lost and forgotten, stored within Sahael and A.M.I.T for the benefit of the Sahaelian and Alkebulan people. To reshare this information, the four royal families must make it back to Sahael first. The six secret bloodlines must be able to travel freely throughout Eastern Aarde."

"Inheritance? Where the great separation took place?" Aamira asked, clearing her throat still.

The light continued shifting from one mirror to the next, though Aamira could have sworn that it was moving faster than before.

Adewara twisted the hair at the end of his beard. "Sahael is also my people's home, but we chose to dwell in Timbuktu until we were forced into exile. We fought over the lands of Inheritance, preventing the Rysallians from taking it. The six sacred bloodlines we sent after the four realms agreed to gather in Sahael once more to determine how Aarde was to be managed. Five of the six bloodlines chose to serve and protect the Alkebulan people. The Orisha, Yoruba, Hausan, Demir, and the Egyptian saw how the Black people were being treated on Aarde, especially in Alkebulan, and wanted to do all that was in their power to protect them no matter the cost. The Lysinnian bloodline into the two lineages: Hornan, and Egyptian. Because they are outside of Sahael and Timbuktu where the Lysinnian bloodline is, they became Hornan scholars who chose not to fight, knowing we needed to help restore Sahael in other ways. The Rysallians, the only witan bloodline, wanted to dominate and subdue the inhabitants of Aarde. This went against what the five tribes wanted, so a skirmish was started for the control and rights to Aarde. After several years of fighting, the Hornan's stayed, while the other five bloodlines were scattered when they returned to Sahael, as the Rysallians migrated into western Aarde."

"Then we need to get your people to Sahael also," Aamira said.

"No," answered Adewara. "For my people to return home to Sahael, the four bloodlines must gather, setting the stage for the first gathering to be completed."

"Wait! So, you can't return home until Sahael is restored?" Yinká asked.

"That's correct," Adewara replied.

"What about Timbuktu?" Abioye asked. "It was once your home away from home. I believe that you and your people can stay and make Timbuktu your home again until the other bloodlines return to Sahacl."

"It's possible," Adewara admitted. "They would need to be

alerted that some of the sacred bloodlines have made it to Sahael
though before they would choose to return to Timbuktu. The signs
of the times are upon us. The currents are changing and shifting as
a result, the seas are dying, and their true color is diminishing. The
Quakes around Aarde are worsening, causing destruction
everywhere that threatens Aardians on either side of the Nibiru
wall. Nearly all the pieces are in place. None of this will be easy.
And don't forget, we still need a representative of the Rysallian
bloodline too. It seems as if we have too many missions in front of
us, keeping Sahael ever farther from our---"

The mirrors suddenly lit up one by one, filling the chamber
with light. At the same time, a high-pitched screech began
emanating from the hanging looking glasses. The sound grew in
intensity, forcing Aamira to cover her ears. Even so, her teeth
seemed to vibrate with the powerful sound.

"What is that noise?" Yekú yelled, holding his hands to his
ears.

"I can feel it in my bones!" Aamira cried.

Adewara looked around in surprise. "It's an alarm of some
type! There must have been a key word that needed to be spoken,
or something needing to be done with the mirrors. I'm unsure!"

Aamira ran to the chamber entrance and looked down the
long hallway and staircase beyond. She saw shadows on the steps
as soldiers came running in response to the deafening sound.

"Narsan soldiers are coming!" she shouted as loudly as
possible.

"Run!" Abioye commanded.

The royal family and Adewara charged into the hallway
and headed back toward the vent they had entered through. As they
turned a corner however, a spear slammed into the wall beside
Yemí's head.

"Intruders!" cried a soldier in silver armor wearing a full-face helmet with slits over the eyes. At least a dozen warriors ran behind the man, all carrying spears as well.

Aamira conjured a glowing green blade and stabbed the lead soldier in the chest.

"Keep going!" she yelled as she pulled the sword back and kicked the man's body toward his fellow soldiers.

The royal family plunged down the stairs toward the lower levels. Horns blew, echoing in the caverns. The sound of iron-shod boots clattered all around as arrows flew in the hallways.

Finally, the family turned a dark corner and saw the vent they had climbed through.

"Climb in!" Aamira ordered.

Yemí jumped into the vent without a word, followed by Yekú and Abioye. As Adewara climbed in, an arrow whizzed through the air and hit him in the shoulder. Adewara cried out in pain, dropping the book into the dark shaft. Aamira turned to see two legions converging on their position, one from the right 50 yards away and one from the left, about the same distance and closing. At least a hundred soldiers shouted and ran at their targets with rage in their eyes. Witan faces grew closer and closer.

Aamira and Adewara locked eyes for a moment as an arrow shattered against the stone wall mere inches from her face. She knew they didn't have enough time for all of them to climb into the vent. Making a decision, Aamira pushed Adewara, and he disappeared into the shaft with a painful cry.

"Keep my family safe!" she yelled after him.

Another arrow bounced off the wall next to Aamira as she grabbed her remaining two sons. She darted across the hall to the short staircase and water inlet where they had bathed less than an hour before. Taking a deep breath, she dove into the salty water and swam as deep as she could. She looked back, seeing Yomí and Yinká dive in behind her. Aamira swam as deep as she could into the brackish water until she felt the pull of the current. A pipe to her left seemed to feed the wash basin directly from the ocean. How long the pipe ran she could only guess, but it was their only means of escape.

Waving to her sons, Aamira swam forward and climbed into the shadowy pipe, which was barely big enough for her to fit. Pushing herself forward, she felt the current strengthen. Still no light appeared in front of her.

Aamira's lungs began to burn in her chest as she swam as best she could in the tight duct. The current pulled faster and faster, but still there was no light.

Unable to hold her breath any longer, Aamira gasped in the water, feeling water fill her throat.

She was about to die.

Her sons were about to die.

She would never make it to Sahael, and thus her people would never be redeemed.

Ishtar and Obatala had chosen the wrong person to save Aarde.

As blackness overcame her senses, Aamira thought of all the people she had left behind and would never see again; Oadira, Heziara, Braémah her guardian from the plantation. So many good people would suffer because of her failure.

She closed her eyes and let death claim another victim.

CHAPTER II
THE LOST & FOUND
BLOODLINE

Aarde, The Nibiru wall, Goree Castle

Aamira coughed as water rushed up from her throat and out her mouth. It felt almost like throwing up, but somehow worse. Her lungs ached and she felt dead, which only confirmed the fact that she was alive.

"Is she going to be, okay?" a young man's voice asked. It was Yinká.

"I think so." That voice was Yomí.

Aamira slowly opened her eyes as she continued hacking and expelling liquid from her lungs. She rolled onto her stomach and vomited as well.

"I heard something over here!" another voice shouted. Aamira didn't recognize this voice.

Yomí leaned close to Aamira and whispered, "You need to be quiet, Mother. They'll find us."

Aamira did her best to keep from retching again and rolled onto her back again. She stared up at the stone ceiling above and gained her bearings for the first time. They were surrounded by large wooden crates that stood at least as tall as her sons. They must be in an unloading area for the ships. Sunlight shone from somewhere on their left through an entryway Aamira could not see from her spot amidst the crates. Water dripped into a puddle nearby and echoed around them. Footsteps drew closer, boots thumping against the stone floor. After a moment they moved farther away, along with voices shouting something Aamira wasn't quite alert enough to understand.

"Where are we?" she asked after a few deep breaths.

"We came out of the pipe among the ships here in the dock," Yomí said as he leaned against the closest crate. "You were limp and unconscious, so we pulled you out of the water and hid here among the boxes and stuff."

Aamira sat up. Her head ached as badly as her chest. "Where are your father and the others? Any sign of them?"

"Not that we've seen," Yinká shrugged.

The three of them sat silent among the crates for the rest of the day as patrols marched by, commanders shouting orders. Aamira listened closely to the conversations of the soldiers just on the other side of the boxes. She heard at one point that some of the intruders were believed to have drowned, while the sewers were being checked for the others. No one ever searched the crates to see if anyone was hiding mere feet away from the Narsan soldiers. They were fools, but Aamira was glad for their stupidity. If they were to be discovered, she would be unable to put up much of a fight.

Darkness fell eventually and Aamira was feeling better by that point. She was hungry, so they crept from their concealment and moved in the dark to find food. They came upon a small crate full of fruit and dried meats, which they ate gratefully.

"We can't stay here," she whispered to her sons as a dozen soldiers unloaded more crates from one of the ships less than twenty feet away.

"Where should we go?" Yinká asked.

Aamira looked up at the stone ceiling twenty feet above. "If we can sneak to the top of the wall, we may be able to see Admiral Abdul's ship once morning hits. By now they would have been sent on to western Aarde, but I doubt they would have sailed far without us. That will be our best chance of finding them."

The rest of the night consisted of her and her sons creeping from shadow to shadow, avoiding guards, and climbing quiet staircases. Eventually they found a series of circular staircases that climbed for a thousand steps each. Eventually they emerged in the fresh air on the top of the wall. A stiff wind blew from the east, never letting up for a moment.

Large brass basins ten feet across stood on the parapets filled with wood and fire, lighting the area. Soldiers stood around the flames warming themselves in the night and laughing about things Aamira could not hear. She and her sons found a deserted corner piled high with rusted chains and coiled rope. There they sat in a corner against the cold Orichalcum metal wall. The surface was not smooth like Aamira had expected, but rather rough and pitted, as if beaten in place by giant sledgehammers. Behind them several openings acted as viewpoints for guardians of the wall, allowing Aamira her first glimpse at western Aarde. No details could be seen in the night, save for the lamplights from ships and what appeared to be a sizable town a thousand feet below.

"I can't believe we are on top of the Nibiru wall," Yomí said quietly. "I learned so much about this place in Timbuktu. Yekú would make me read about it out loud to him while he cooked in the kitchens."

"Tell me about some of the things you read," Aamira said, imagining her two sons reading together as Yekú cooked his favorite meals for them in the Timbuktu kitchens.

"The Nibiru wall stretches over half of Aarde," Yomí began. "It extends through the lands of the Inheritance, Dale

Island, and halfway through the untamed lands of Nazaum. The Nibiru wall was the only way to gain access to either side of Aarde. The only other way Aardians could get into the new and old world or be forced to travel across Nazaum, nearly 800 miles long and 400 miles wide of untamed land.

"The Nibiru were responsible for protecting the old world and the new world from each other by only allowing traders, merchants, and missionaries into western Aarde. Before the Nibiru could fully take control of their sacred duty, They disappeared. As a result, the Narsans took control of the Nibiru wall."

The sky to the east started to lighten. Aamira dozed as best she could until the sun rose. The fires in the brass basins were extinguished and the guards dispersed at the end of the third watch. All was quiet.

Aamira stood and stretched her legs. The top of the wall was wider than she expected; at least 50 feet across. She could see for several miles in each direction, though the wall followed the contours of the land and would rise and fall in a series of steps and slopes. No soldiers patrolled in their area now though, allowing her and the boys a chance to look around.

"See if there is any food anywhere," she told her sons as she looked out on western Aarde. The ocean hugged the coast below next to the city she had seen in the night. It was indeed large, with a dozen sailing ships docked along the port. She saw no sign of the impressive vessel from Timbuktu, however. Where had Admiral Abdul gone?

A shout brought Aamira's attention back to the wall. She and the boys ducked behind the ropes once again as a cadre of soldiers ran past shouting about a guard being found stabbed on the stairs.

Aamira turned to Yomí. "You didn't kill anyone, did you?"

"I barely made it twenty feet from you trying to find food," he answered. "No, I didn't kill anyone, Mother."

"I didn't either," Yinká said.

The soldiers disappeared down the stairs and a nervous quiet returned to the wall. The wind continued blowing fiercely as it had through the night.

Something scraped against the metal of the wall less than ten feet away, followed by what sounded like quick footsteps coming closer to them. Aamira looked at her sons as she formed a vibrant emerald dagger in her right hand. Placing her finger over her lips to make sure they remained quiet; she prepared to attack if necessary.

"Empress Adesola," a man's voice whispered. "High King Yinká? Prince Yemí?"

Aamira recognized the voice. She stood. "Adewara?"

The Educator stood up and smiled. His graying beard whipped around in the wind and his afro shook as if the breeze would pull it from his head. His left shoulder slumped slightly where the arrow had hit him, but it was bandaged and looked clean.

"It's me," Adewara grinned. He stepped forward and embraced Aamira and the boys. "I am so glad to have found you!"

"Have you been tracking us?" Aamira asked.

"I have."

"Where is Abioye and the other boys?" Aamira asked as she pulled Adewara back to where they had been hiding. "Are they okay?"

"They made it to the ship without being detected," Adewara explained. "I ordered Admiral Abdul to continue sailing toward Inheritance for their own safety. Right before we got on the ship, the orders were being shouted to search all the ships in the surrounding towns to see if anything was out of place. The soldiers tried to stop Abdul from sailing away because they had never seen a ship like his before. Apparently while we were searching for the castle, the Narsan guards tried to arrest Abdul and his crew so they could seize the ship for themselves. Only through Abdul convincing them that an army of soldiers waited below deck to defend the vessel did the Narsans back off. It was about that time when the alarm sounded, and all hell broke loose. I told Abdul to keep sailing no matter what and we would find a way to catch up. I then jumped overboard and started looking for you."

"Abioye and the boys stayed behind on the ship?" Aamira asked. Sadness and disappointment twisted her stomach. Had her husband and sons abandoned her?

"Only because I gave them no other choice," Adewara said. "I charged Abioye and your sons with uniting my people on Inheritance. They will only follow someone of the royal bloodline, which meant the Emperor and the princes needed to lead the expedition. Abioye made me promise to bring you all back safely, and I intend to fulfill that promise."

"How's your shoulder?" Yomí asked.

Adewara shifted his arm and grimaced. "I did my best to keep it from getting dirty in the sewers as we made our way back to the vessel. Luckily after I swam back to the castle once we sailed off, I found medical supplies in a wooden cabinet. I was able to sterilize the wound and pack it well enough. As long as I can make a healing poultice with some herbs over the next few days, I should heal well enough."

Yomí slumped back against the metal wall and blew out a deep breath. "So now what do we do? The ship is sailing to Inheritance, and we have no way to get there, or even to get off this wall. I mean, the stairs are covered in guards now since someone was killed, I guess."

A small smile pulled at Adewara's lips.

"You, did it?" Aamira asked, almost laughing. "You killed a guard on the steps to the top of the wall.

Adewara shrugged, followed by a painful scowl. "Damn, this shoulder hurts. And yes, I was discovered by a sentry about twenty minutes ago and had to silence him before he cried out and alerted everyone else to my presence. Unfortunately, I didn't have anywhere to hide the body."

"Great," Yinká rolled his eyes. "Now more soldiers are going to come up here to find out who killed their man. We have nowhere to go."

Holding up a finger, Adewara smiled. "And that is where you're wrong, young High King Yinká. I tracked you through the night from where you had been hiding among the crates because I smelled where someone had vomited."

"That was me," Aamira admitted, holding up her hand.

"She almost drowned," Yomí said.

"In any case," Adewara continued, "While I was tracking as best I could in the dark, I found there are shafts that go from the dungeons all the way up here to facilitate air flow. I could look up at the stars from down in the basements. All we need to do is find one and we can descend quickly and have a bit more freedom to explore. We stick to the original plan and see if we can find any members of the Rysallian bloodline. If they're in the dungeons, it's a good bet they're fighting against the Narsans, which would make them more likely to help us."

Since no better plans became apparent, Aamira, Adewara, Yomí and Yinká began searching for the air shafts. Several patrols marched by over the next hour, forcing them to hide multiple times, but eventually Adewara found what he was looking for. Steam rose from a pillar on the western side of the wall about twenty feet from the top.

"That's one of the shafts, right there," Adewara pointed.

"How do we get down there?" Yinká asked.

Aamira smiled and jumped over the side, sliding down the wall to the vent and landing on the top easily. It was five feet square, making enough room for at least one more person to stand beside her. Unlike the grate on top of the sewer entrance they had found the day before, the iron bars pulled easily away from the metal housing because they weren't mortared in place, likely because no one ever thought someone would try to sneak down from the top of the wall in this way.

From there, Aamira and the others shimmied their way down the stone vent by pressing their backs to one side and their legs to the other. The interior of the shaft was three-feet-by-three-feet square; cramped, but big enough that they could still fit. The air was humid and stuffy, leaving a layer of sweat on Aamira's body thick enough to drip into her eyes from her forehead.

It took them at least an hour to reach the dungeons below. Aamira lost track of time once they could no longer see the light above them from the entry point.

Aamira climbed out of the shaft and into a small alcove in the dimly lit dungeons. Stifling air surrounded her, smelling of urine and other foul stenches she didn't want to contemplate. Torches blazed from their housings on the stone walls, glinting off iron bars. A series of cells, spaced every ten feet, filled the opposite wall. Aamira glanced quickly but didn't see any prisoners in the cells she could see from the recess by the vent exit. Deep shadows filled the dungeons, which would be to their advantage if they needed to move about. Aamira stepped out of the alcove and jumped at the sight of a Narsan soldier, but he was asleep in a chair halfway down the hall.

"There's a guard over there," she whispered to Adewara as he climbed out of the shaft.

Just then, Aamira heard shouting from down the arched hallway. She glanced around a pillar next to the vent so she couldn't be seen. Two soldiers stepped out of a cell, obviously frustrated. The man in the chair quickly woke up and stood at attention.

"I told you they was in there, Cargil," one of the men yelled at the other. "Don't you think I would have noticed if one of our prisoners had escaped?"

"I don't know what the hell you do down here," the man Cargil replied, poking his finger into the chest of the other soldier. "All I know is the two of them have escaped you before and killed several of my men."

"Well, they didn't do it today, Cargil."

"Somebody did!" Cargil screamed. "I got a man stabbed on the stairs near the top of the wall, magic alarms going off, and ships escaping before being searched. I don't know what the hell is going on, but if I find those two who broke free again, I'll have you hanged right along with them!"

The two men continued arguing as they turned the corner on the far side of the hall, voices echoing. The guard walked over and locked the cell door the men had exited, before sitting back down in his chair and closing his eyes again.

"What was that all about?" Yomí asked, voice quiet.

"The guards think some of the prisoners were the ones to kill the man upstairs and set off the alarm," Adewara answered. "They don't seem to think it was anyone from the outside. That's good."

Adewara motioned for Aamira and the princes to follow him as he hugged close to the wall and moved away from the resting guard. As they approached a torch, Adewara moved swiftly just in case any guards wandered toward them. After turning a corner, they entered an area with no cells, only a wooden door with the Narsan symbol carved haphazardly into it. Adewara slowly opened the door and stepped inside. After a moment, he popped his head out and nodded for the others to join him inside.

The room was spacious, with high ceilings. A large fireplace blazed with flames in the corner, offering the only light in the windowless hovel. A table and chairs centered the room, covered in scrolls and maps.

"Is this some sort of meeting room?" Yinká asked.

"It looks like it," Adewara said as he rifled through the documents on the table. He picked up several pages and pointed to a red stamp of the Rysallian sigil of an eagle's head with wings coming out of its back. "There are some documents here with the Rysallian symbol on them."

"What do they say?" Aamira questioned.

"Why do they have the symbol on them?" Yomí asked.

Adewara examined one page and then the next, eyes moving rapidly. "It looks like they stamp the bloodline of all prisoners held in the dungeons. Look over there. I see one with an Orishan sigil stamped on it."

Aamira looked at the documents quickly. "Why would they do that?"

"I don't know," Adewara admitted. "I assume that prisoners kept here in the wall are high value targets. They're meant to be shipped off somewhere else or wait for someone more important to come take them off the Narsans hands."

"Like Natas?" Yomí asked.

Adewara continued reading through all the documents without answering. "There's a pedigree chart here with the documents. It looks like they indeed have some Rysallian prisoners here waiting to be transferred. From the dates, it looks like they've been here for…awhile."

"Who are they?" Aamira asked.

"Ryland and his son Ryal." Adewara said as he opened and read the parchment papers. "This reads that Ryland and his son Ryal, and three of his daughters, were betrothed to the leaders of the Trinity to unify and solidify their blood right and their claim to Eastern Aarde. Apparently Rylands wife was killed after birthing Ryal, their youngest child. This shows that their three daughters, Reanna, Rhiannon, and Rayna, were married within the trinity bloodlines several centuries ago. They were married to the Viscount, the Chancellor, and the Head. This allowed the Trinity to combine and merge bloodlines with the Trinity, solidifying and giving Lord Commander Natas complete control of the Rysallian sacred bloodline through the chosen right of election."

"Wait," Yinká interrupted. "Centuries ago? Like this Ryland is of the old blood?"

"Yes," Adewara confirmed. "I've actually heard his name before. He was quite important to Natas before the fall of Sahael. He himself was once a king here on the wall."

Looking down at the documents in Adewara's hand, Aamira shook her head. "So why are he and his son in the dungeons? If he was important to Natas and helped him 100 years ago to put his plans into motion, why would the Narsans have him locked up?"

"I think we should find out." Adewara said. "We should

sneak into their cell and talk to them. If they are here because they are fighting against Natas, that would be a huge boon to us."

"Or maybe they just pissed Natas off, or tried to overthrow him," Yomí said with a shrug. "Just because they're here in the dungeons doesn't mean they're on our side."

"Very true, Prince Yomí," Adewara conceded. "Still, talking to them is our best option. Remember, the Rysallians weren't always our enemies. They were our brothers once, despite the color of their skin being different. No one cared about such trivial things in the ancient days. They were protectors of the wall here. The Narsans used their airships to force the Nibiru into hiding rather than surrender by dropping nitrate obsidian bombs that didn't affect the wall at all but forced them into fleeing. They took control away from the Rysallians still in service to the old order."

As they moved toward the door, Aamira remembered something Adewara had said about how Natas took control of Eastern Aarde. "Lord Commander Natas used the right of election to gain control over the Trinity."

"The same way you were able to do it," Adewara said. "He knows the laws and traditions better than anyone. He knows how to manipulate. He promised the Trinity they'd have a chance to prosper and spread the Nauthian Gospel for control of Eastern Aarde within the sacred bloodline. Let's be quiet and careful out there."

Yinká grabbed Adewara's robes quickly and held up his finger. "Why not have Mother skin-change into one of the guards. She has this ability and has done it before. My brother and I never have. Wouldn't that make things easier?"

Aamira shivered at the thought of making an incredibly painful transformation for such a limited reason.

"You've never used the ability," Aamira repeated. "If you had, you would realize how excruciating such a transformation can be. I will only use it when there are no other options, and only then, in the direst need. Plus, it's been many years since I've skin-changed. Not since before any of you boys were born. I would need to practice and now is not the time. Let's go."

The door creaked quietly as Adewara poked his head out to see if any soldiers patrolled the dungeon hallway. He nodded and stepped out, followed by Aamira, Yomí, and Yinká. They quickly made their way back toward where the two soldiers had been arguing. There, still sleeping in his chair, was the remaining soldier.

"We need to make sure he stays asleep," Aamira said.

"I got it, Mother," Yomí grinned. Silently he jumped forward from the shadows, forming a glowing green hammer in his hands, and smashed the guard over the head with it. The man slumped and fell onto the floor without a sound.

"I didn't mean crush his skull!" Aamira said as they walked over.

Yomí lifted the man and placed him back in the chair. "He'll be fine. He'll just wake up with a bit of a headache is all."

Adewara removed the set of keys from the guard's belt and unlocked the cell door that the two soldiers had exited earlier. They walked into the dark space, smelling feces and sweat. The cell seemed to go further back into the shadows, but Aamira couldn't be sure how big the space actually was.

Using her natural dark vision, Aamira saw two people lying in the closest corner near the entrance, arms and legs chained to the wall. They were both male, with witan skin covered in dirt and scabs. Long blond hair came down past their shoulders and they both wore ragged beards, as if it had been years since they had shaven.

Adewara knelt and shook the closest man lightly. The bearded man startled awake and pulled away as if ready for a blow.

"Who are you?!" the man cried. "We didn't escape! Don't harm anyone here."

"It's just the two of you," Yomí mumbled.

"Are you Ryland and Ryal?" Adewara asked.

The second man sat up and blinked. "I am Ryal. This is my father Ryland."

"Who are you?" the older man, Ryland asked again.

"I am Empress Aamira Adesola of the Yoruban bloodline," Aamira answered. "I am seeking the redemption of Sahael. Would you stand in my way or serve me in this endeavor? Answer quickly!"

Ryland's eyes began to water. His head slumped into his hands as he wept. Deep sobs echoed in the darkness.

"Is it true?" he asked, still crying. "Has redemption come for me and my family? Will our sins be forgiven after a century of grief and repentance?"

"What's he talking about?" Yinká asked his brother.

"Did you betray our people?" Aamira asked Ryland without answering her son's question.

"I did," Ryland sobbed. "Natas made promises of power and peace, of all people returning to live with Ishtar and Obatala if his plans came to fruition. We believed him and went along. Only after several decades did it become clear we had been deceived. Many of my people didn't care at that point because they had wealth and power, but those of us of royal blood who live for centuries, we understood our folly. By then, it was too late."

"You've fought against Natas?" Adewara asked, still crouched next to the chained men.

"Yes, we have," Rylan replied. "Natas punished our family. My stepmother is dead. My sisters are dead. I haven't seen them in the flesh for many decades."

"We seek redemption," Ryland cried. "We seek the return of the chosen houses. We seek the fall of Natas the deceiver."

Aamira nudged her sons. "Cut through their chains. We'll take them with us. If what they say is true, they will have no problem fighting beside us and proving it."

Ryland held up his manacled hands. "The others! The others must be released too." He pointed toward the darkness on the far side of the cell. "They need to be released as well. Please! Save them too!"

As if responding to the old man's words. Footsteps echoed from the darkness.

"It's okay to come out," Ryland shouted. "She is of the Yoruban Royal House. I told you we would be forgiven and return to the sacred lands."

Witan people began stepping out of the darkness into what little light the torches outside the cell provided. Dozens emerged, with more still making their way forward.

"By Ishtar," Adewara breathed.

Now aware of the other people in the cell, Aamira focused on the newcomers. At least a hundred other people emerged from the cramped quarters of what turned out to be a larger group cell than she had expected. The people were a mix of dark skinned and light skinned people. The black prisoners were obviously of Sahaelian descent by their size. Most of them were gaunt and weak, but the remnants of their heritage still burned in their eyes.

"Who are these other prisoners?" Aamira asked.

"My people," Ryland replied, wiping his tears and smiling. "The Rysallian bloodline. The adults that were captured during the fall of our last fortress. All the children were slaughtered."

Yinká leaned closer to Adewara. "I swear you said the Rysallians were the only witan bloodline."

"That's correct," Adewara said, standing back up.

"Then why are more than half of these people black?" Aamira asked.

"They are the Blacks who were cast out of the Rysallian bloodline," Ryal said.

Ryland stood, letting his chains clink against each other. He was seven feet tall, far taller than most witan men Aamira had met in her life.

"They wanted to exterminate all Black Rysallians," Ryland said. "Seeing them as a stain on the witan bloodline. I had married a black woman after Ryal's mother passed away. She then gave birth to my daughters, all of which carried the darker skin of their mother. Many of us had mixed our bloodlines over the centuries, seeing no problem with the practice. Lord Commander Natas ordered the remaining witans in the Bloodline to take out the Blacks who share the same lineage, just not the same skin color. We refused. My daughters were married for the chosen right of election to witan suiters. It was all a trap. It was rumored that their witan husbands killed my four daughters and took their power for themselves."

Yomí reached over and took Ryland's chained hands into his own. He formed a pick and stuck it between the links, twisting until the rusted metal popped and broke. He then did the same for Ryal.

"Thank you for saving us, and our king," one of the Black Rysallian men said in a raspy and weak voice.

"Thank you," another Black Rysallian said from the crowd. The Black prisoners all stood six feet tall, with brown eyes, and black wooly hair. The witans had similar features to Ryland, with dirty blonde hair and teeth.

After being released from his restraints, Ryland walked over to the other prisoners and embraced several of them. He turned to Aamira and the princes. "These Blacks are all that's left of the denied Rysallian Bloodline. There was a section of Blacks that were blessed by Ibeji with the sacred blood of the chosen and the ancients. These Blacks were blessed with Aventurine colored eyes linking them to the Ancient Bloodline."

The cell suddenly blazed with green light as the prisoners manifested their glowing eyes, similar in brightness to Aamira's family's irises. were lit up allowing Empress Adesola to stand up where she immediately noticed Ryland and Ryal's Aventurine emerald-colored eyes of her children Prince Yomí and King Yinká.

Ryland and Ryal then stepped forward and kneeled before Aamira. Many of the prisoners kneeled as well, tears in their eyes.

"We seek forgiveness, Empress Adesola," Ryland said. "We will prove our fidelity in any way you see fit, even if it be we sacrifice our lives for our fellow prisoners. Our sins are many, but we know Ishtar and Obatala are forgiving to the penitent."

"Stand," Aamira said, motioning with her hand for them to rise from their knees. "There will be no blood sacrifice today, or ever in my presence. If you wish to join us in the redemption of Sahael, your actions will speak louder than any word you could speak."

Tears came to Ryland's eyes again as he stood before Aamira. "We have been fighting for half a century. So, few of us remain. My son and I have been held captive in the wall on and off for the past 33 years hoping for a changing of the tide. We would escape, fight back, and be captured yet again. A year ago, our fellow Rysallians were taken captive as well. Our last fortress finally fell. Natas wishes us to rot in these walls for eternity as punishment. He will yet fall; of that I have no doubt. He wishes to take away all choice from the inhabitants of Aarde."

"Can you help us?" Ryal asked, looking at Yinká and Yomí.

"Yes," Yinká nodded. "We can track down Admiral Abdul's ship and he can transport them wherever they need to go, or perhaps back to Sahael with us."

"Perhaps, but Admiral Abdul is on his way to Inheritance to Adewara's people," Yomí said.

"He is indeed," Adewara agreed. "Admiral Abdul is currently on his way to Inheritance to retrieve the people and take them back to Timbuktu."

"But they need to come to Sahael with us, right?" Yomí questioned.

Adewara shook his head. "Not all of them."

"What do you mean?" Aamira asked, confused. "We need Rysallian representation with us if we are to reclaim Sahael. You're the one who told us that."

"But you'll remember," Adewara said, finger raised like a primary school teacher, "Abioye reminded us of the Nairobi Laws. If a witan is brought to Sahael, the Signs of the Times will no longer protect the chosen bloodlines. I've been pondering the meaning of this since that initial discussion back in the library of Timbuktu. Now we have our answer."

"Are you saying if we bring a witan into Sahael, the

bloodlines could lose the protection of the signs?" Yinká asked.

"This is what I truly fear," Adewara said.

"You can take the Black Rysallians back to Sahael," Ryland said. "Ryal and myself, and any other witan will stay behind in prison so long as we know the redemption is coming."

"So, we just leave them here, to fend for themselves as we leave?" Yomí asked.

"Yes," Adewara said.

"Stop this! We're no better than Lord Commander Natas if we leave people behind to suffer merely because of the color of their skin," Aamira shouted. "Isn't this how the great dispersal on Aarde started? We need to find a compromise that doesn't involve leaving others to die."

Ryland knelt once more before Aamira. "Our fates are in your hands."

Prophecies and revelations had been the bane of Aamira's existence since her childhood. Adewara and all the true believers always pointed to prophecy as the purest form of knowledge. And yet, prophecy hadn't saved Sahael from being destroyed. Prophecy hadn't rescued slaves or stopped Natas from rising to power. People based all their decisions on what they interpreted a prophecy to mean, that they took away their own agency as effectively as Natas would. Aamira would have none of that. She believed Ishtar and Obatala had a plan, and that she was indeed part of that plan, but she would not limit her choices merely because a prophecy could be interpreted one way or the other.

"You are all under my rule for the time being," Aamira said. "Whatever prophecy contradicts or agrees with whatever other prophecy; I will not leave anyone to suffer and die. Everyone comes with us. That means we need to leave this place prepared to track down Admiral Abdul's ship, and the rest of my family. We need to gain control of this castle. We have the numbers now, and we can use these numbers to overtake the guards and regain control. We'll be attacking from the inside, which they will be totally unprepared for. They will fall quickly and easily with so many of us catching them by surprise. Who's ready to fight?"

A cheer filled the cell loud enough for any nearby guards to hear. No one seemed to care. A fight was about to start, and they seemed more than ready to face death if needed.

The first assault had been a covert maneuver to take control of the dungeons of Goree Castle. After that though, all-out war commenced. After finding a cache of weapons, the Rysallians fought like dragons against their oppressors, led by Aamira and her sons.

The Narsan SS fought back for four days trying to regain complete control of the Nibiru wall. In the end, not a single soldier was left alive so that word of the assault would not reach the ears of other armies.

During the fight, Aamira watched her sons Yomí, and Yinká, use their Yoruban gifts effortlessly, conjuring Egyptian glaive swords and manifesting protective shield barriers that turned their skin indestructible. For her part, Aamira had used her abilities to shake the ground many times, bringing the Narsan soldiers to heel with fear.

On the morning of the fifth day, all was quiet along the wall, and Aamira had slept well for the first time in weeks. Everyone gathered in the courtyard at first light.

"Thank you for saving us once again from slaughter," Ryland said to Aamira in front of his people. Since she had last seen him, Ryland had bathed, trimmed his blond beard, and now wore Narsan armor with the 'N' symbol of Natas removed and replaced with a bent piece of metal in a haphazard Rysallian sigil of the Liger. Other Rysallians had done the same, and the less than two hundred of them that survived now looked like a true fighting force.

"We are eternally indebted to you," Ryal said, bowing to the royal family. He too had washed and wore a crimson cape. Ryal had completely shaved his beard and now looked quite handsome.

Adewara stepped forward. "Empress, we have limited Rysallian forces to hold this section of wall, but with the castle now under our control, it will be difficult for the Narsans to retake it so long as we are vigilant. We captured their supplies and now have enough food for many months, and it will be months before more Narsans can arrive and attempt to occupy the wall once more. In the meantime, the royal family should meet with Ryland and Ryal to discuss future plans. Shall we reconvene in the upper magistrate's office?"

Aamira followed Adewara up a flight of stairs to an office with a balcony overlooking the ocean. It had obviously been used by someone important who was now dead. They wouldn't mind if the Yoruban Royal family commandeered the space. Aamira, her sons, Adewara, Ryland and Ryal sat at a conference table that still had several loves of stale bread on platters from before they had launched their surprise attack. The princes both sat down while the others remained standing.

Adewara turned to Ryland. "Please explain to us what happened with Natas all those years ago."

"The Rysallian Bloodline was set up and lied to by Lord

Commander Natas after phylacteries were given to every Rysallian," Ryland began. "When the phylacteries didn't have the intended effect to control and suppress the Black Rysallians, the witans in the Rysallian bloodline were ordered to kill them, creating a Dyad in the Rysallian Bloodline, rendering the witan side null and void."

"How could you allow Lord Commander Natas to make two distinct bloodlines?" Adewara asked, leaning on his elbows.

"The people were tricked," Ryal said. "It wasn't our plan. Natas simply lured us into a false sense of security and over decades slowly took complete control over who could breed with whom."

Adewara seemed unconvinced. "You created two separate bloodlines that have caused untold amounts of destruction. Due to your negligence, you have set in motion a series of events that are not reversible. All Aarde will have to suffer through it until the ramifications have played out. I know Empress Adesola wishes to grant mercy to you and the remaining witans in your bloodline, the truth is only the Blacks in the Rysallian heritage hold the rightful claim to return to Sahael. Witans such as yourself don't have the privilege. It was forsaken the day you followed Lord Commander Natas. He used your history and skin color to manipulate your bloodlines, creating division and deceiving you all. The right of Election resides with the Blacks in the Rysallian bloodline that belong in Sahael."

"It's not right," Aamira said, stomping her foot like she would as a child. "The Rysallians were deceived. Many of them continue with Natas as their leader to this day, but the witan men and women here have fought and suffered for their repentance."

"I cannot deny the truth of the law," Adewara replied. "I know a representative of the Rysallian bloodline must be with us to save Sahael and reform the Sentinel Islands into one landmass, but not all of them. We need not burden us all with their crimes."

Aamira shook her head. "I don't live by prophecies that could be interpreted a hundred different ways. And laws can be changed. I say we take everyone with us and let us stand before Ishtar and Obatala not as Natas would, having denied what is right because of how a person looks."

Adewara looked from Aamira to Ryal. His eyelids twitched as if battling against his will.

"So be it," Adewara said. "I am a believer in prophecy and the law. However, I will go along with this if the witans forsake their claims forever to any lands in Sahael. If allowed by the Gods to stay because of their repentance, they will live as guests only." He turned to Ryland. "Do you agree to this?"

"I do," Ryland said with a bow. "We will make no claim on Sahaelian lands. To take part in the redemption of the free peoples will be our reward, and a hope of our forgiveness."

Just then, one of the Rysallian guards ran into the office. Sweat dripped from his dark chin.

"Empress," he gasped. "Since the battle, more and more ships have lined up on both sides of the wall seeking to pass through. We have barred the way as per your orders, but the crews are becoming belligerent and violent, particularly toward our black brothers. We don't have the men to hold them off if they decide to push through or attack."

"Damn," Aamira whispered. She knew ships would still be seeking passage but figured a delay of a day or two while they figured out how to keep control of the wall wouldn't cause too many problems. The thought hadn't occurred to her about what would happen when dozens of vessels were all held up at once, with angry witans at the helm.

"Are there any signs of Narsan ships in the area?" Yomí

asked as he stood up at the table.

"No, sir," the guard answered. "But we have no idea how long it will take more Narsan forces to arrive. Right now, we're afraid we'll be overrun simply by the sailors seeking entrance to western Aarde."

"What about---" Yomí began.

Aamia raised her hand to cut off any further speaking. "My sons and I will descend to the tunnel entrance. If any witan sailors want a fight, we can give it to them. Continue securing the wall. Even with a small number of us, we should still be able to defend ourselves effectively within the fortifications. Have courage. No one will ever take away what we have reclaimed. Not while I draw breath."

CHAPTER III
A DYAD IN THE BLOODLINE

Western Aarde, The Nibiru wall,

Boats approached the Nibiru wall unceasingly over the next two days, waiting for admittance to Eastern Aarde. The longer the boats had to wait, the more hostile and angry they became. Aamira and her sons had effectively cowed many of them, but the abundant resources of the nautical trade brought more and more ships, which then felt emboldened to stand against the new magistrates of the wall. The witans and Aardians shouted from their ships with spies amongst them in the boats.

"There are a lot of witans trying to get to the other side of the wall to the Sovereign lands," Ryal said as Aamira and Yinká stood watch over the logjam from a nearby parapet. The midday sun shone brightly against a cloudless sky. A stiff wind blew from the ocean.

"My mother refuses to allow passage to the witans," Yinká said, eyes locked on two ships that had collided in the cue. Sailors screamed at each other from the opposing decks, each blaming the other for the mishap. "The gates are closed. Alkebulan will not be exploited more than it already has been."

"These people seem harmless to an extent," Ryal said. "Few of them have weapons."

"We've already killed a dozen sailors who swam up to the wall and attacked with stones," Aamira replied, back ridged. The wind caught her long braids and blew them into her face. "If we can disrupt the trade between east and west, the Narsans supply chain will be heavily impacted. Their ability to attack effectively will be curtailed. We have no idea when Admiral Abdul and my husband will make it back here. Until then, we need to hold this location. I cannot reach Sahael without the rest of my family. For now, we wait and do our best to clog the gears of witan dominance."

Several Rysallian soldiers dressed in Narsan armor ran on the stone causeway two stories below and shouted up at the royals.

"Send word to Empress Adesola! An attack is imminent!" one of them cried.

"I'm here," Aamira called down with a wave. "What's happening?"

"A small elite group of Narsan seals from Narsa was just seen on a pair of swift cruiser vessels near the back of the cue, my empress. They have been talking to one of the ships that was sent away at the gate. One cruiser appears to be advancing, weapons at the ready, while the other has sailed south along the wall."

"Thank you!" Yinká shouted. "Spread the word. We'll discuss our options up here."

"Yes, Prince Yinká!"

"What are they capable of?" Aamira asked Ryal as the guards ran beneath the tunnel entry. "You have a lot of experience fighting these types of naval forces. What are we looking at?"

Ryal wiped sweat from his brow and nervously ran his

fingers through his wooly blond locked hair. "The Narsan seals are employed to track the Blacks in the Rysallian bloodline. They are highly trained and conditioned. Once in a fight they don't sleep or eat. All they want to do is wipe out anyone who stands in their way. The Narsan seals kidnap and force Black Rysallians into enslavement and then they rename them. Only through will power, faith, and courage are Black Rysallians able to endure. The Narsans then send them to the 'Arth Nations and the States to be sold into slavery You can see why my father and I have fought so hard these last 30 years, spending more than half of that in the dungeon between escapes."

"That's disgusting!" Aamira spat. "If they attack, what are we looking at from an offensive standpoint?"

"The Narsan seals will attack this wall with catapults, trebuchets, and ballista on floating structures," Ryal answered.

Yinká scoffed. "There's only one small cruiser according to the guards. We can handle that easily. They don't have any of the equipment you're talking about."

"One of the cruisers sailed south," Ryal reminded. "That is a very bad sign. I would bet reinforcements are here within the next day. Two at the most. Even a single legion of say 40 seals would be devastating to our forces here. The seals will fight to the death and do whatever it takes to breach these walls looking for creative ways to neutralize our defenses. The Narsan seals will climb up these walls like spiders. They assaulted our fortress four years ago, right before my father and I were captured the last time. It was terrifying. The only defense that works is a clear oil we spread on the fortress walls. As it drips down, the seals will be unable to ascend. Plus, when the oil touches the water, a black color will start to form, circling around the boats."

"Adewara has told me of this oil before," Yinká said, rubbing the stubble on his young chin. "It was known as the Water

Ash by the ancients."

Ryal smiled. "Yes, we can then throw torches at the black oil creating fire ash on the water. When that happens, it will provide the Nibiru wall with the protection we need to avoid being overrun by these elite fighters."

Aamira turned from the ocean and made her way toward the stairs. "If you know how to make this oil, get your people on it immediately. We need as much of it as you can make. Until Admiral Abdul returns with my husband, we will hold this position."

"I will have what few alchemists remain among us get started immediately, Empress."

The wind blew against Aamira's back as she walked under the stone archway and down the stairs.

They had taken the castle and surrounding wall from the Narsans. They were not going to lose it.

As Ryal had predicted, Narsan seal forces attacked at dusk the following day, taking advantage of the growing darkness and fatigue of their targets. Luckily, the Rysallians had been able to craft enough of the Water Ash oil to dump on the soldiers as they tried to scale the wall. On top of that, hundreds of sailors from the stalled ships had joined the fight. Bodies lay everywhere and floated in the waves. Aamira and her sons, along with Ryal and Ryland, had successfully pushed back a frontal assault on the main tunnel and gates, but Ryal had been correct when he talked about the tenacity of these seals. Nothing seemed to deter their assault.

But then came the fire.

Just before dawn, Aamira ordered archers from the top of the wall to fire flaming arrows into the water. By now the oil had time to spread, coating the hulls of many of the ships. A blaze went up like the sun at noon day. Every boat and ship was engulfed by fire, wiping out nearly all the vessels seeking passage through the Nibiru gates. The remaining ships backed away from the Nibiru wall to preserve themselves, their cargo, and above all their vessels.

The fire burned for four days.

But on the morning of the fifth day, the flames had died.

No more oil was left.

Smoke rose from the water as Aamira looked down from the top of the wall. A thousand feet below, three more Narsan ships had arrived in the night. Yinká and Yomí stood next to her. While the fighting had been sporadic, fatigue set in, nonetheless.

"Ensign Rommel of the Narsan has sent a message, Empress," a witan Rysallian guard said to Aamira as he ran up next to her.

"What does the bastard have to say?" Aamira asked.

"This conflict needs to be ended quickly," the guard informed. "The Ensign then said that if we don't surrender, he will deploy Narsan gliders that have just arrived. He claims they now have over 100 Narsan seals ready for the assault. The Narsan gliders will drop Nitrate bombs on us."

Aamira looked up and down the wall. She and her boys had taken the brunt of the attacks and held their own just fine, but she knew casualties had been suffered among the Rysallians.

"What of our losses, soldier?" she asked.

"Between the arrow assault on the front gates and that

cadre of Narsans that climbed up on the north side of the wall, we've suffered about 20 casualties. That may not sound like much, but it's ten percent of our entire population, Empress, male and female."

"It appears this Ensign Rommel will not give up," Aamira said, hitting her hand against the orichalcum parapet beside her.

"Ensign Rommel helped Lord Commander Natas gain control of Western Aarde," the soldier informed. "Ensign Rommel has been in a few battles and can handle himself. Use caution. He's dangerous."

"Mirgen is correct," Ryal said as he approached Aamira from behind. She turned to see the blonde man, weary and bruised. "He has been a presence in these lands for 200 years. Rommel is of the old blood as well. A nasty man that has completely turned himself over to Natas."

"Tell me more about him," Aamira said, looking down again as the Narsan ships that sailed closer to the wall.

"Ensign Rommel kidnapped Black children from the 'Arth Nations, the States 'Or and the D.I.M.-T.I.M. Nations. Ensign Rommel threatened all the children, holding daggers to their throats, forcing their parents to bend to the will of their governments."

"Why?" Yinká asked.

"This was his way of dividing and conquering," Ryal replied, wiping sweat from his brow. "This allowed Ensign Rommel to break the Black people's spirits and the Black governments he was fighting against. He did this in all the cities to bring the Blacks to their knees. Obsidian Nitrate became his weapon of choice, using it in his catapults to destroy each state's forts and defenses in their respective cities. Ensign Rommel was able to rebuild and control every fort within the nations and the states that are now enslavement strongholds for trafficking, the organ trade, and the enforcement of the Blight Curse."

"You were there for all of this?" Yomí asked.

Yes," Ryal said. "We fought back, but by that time Natas had so much control, we were barely a resistance force. Still, the campaign took Ensign Rommel four years to bring them all under his rule. He was given the right to act under his own authority. There was a lot of blood spilled. Many joined our cause when they saw the destruction, but generations had gotten used to the power and would no longer listen to those of us who had lived for many lifetimes."

"It was Ensign Rommel's charge to uphold and save all of Aardiankind in the name of Ishtar and Obatala's children," the witan guard, Mirgen, added. "Ensign Rommel feels he needs to unite them all under one cause to get them back into their presence one day as his promise to Lord Commander Natas."

Just then, Adewara climbed the stairs to the top of the wall carrying a basket of bread. He handed loaves to the waiting soldiers and ended at Aamira's side.

"The bread is fresh," Adewara said, handing loaves to Aamira and the princes. "Some of the women have been using the kitchens to great effect.

"I wish Yekú was down there with them," Yomí lamented. He took a bite of bread and shrugged. "It's not bad. A bit of cinnamon would go a long way. Yekú would have made it better."

Aamira took a bite of the dry bread and had to agree with her son. It would keep her alive, but there would be little enjoyment in eating it.

Adewara smiled. "Your brother will be able to cook fine meals to your heart's content once our people are safe in Sahael. Until then, enjoy the fruits of other's skill. And I'm fairly certain we don't have any cinnamon."

"How are things at the gate?" Aamira asked.

"The Narsans are preparing for an assault now that the fires have died," Adewara answered. "The Rysallians are brave. They've known war for centuries. They'll fight to the last breath. Ryland is down at the gate ready to kill more Naran seals. I think the man has slaughtered a dozen all by himself."

"Were you down there when Rommel's message arrived?"

"I was," Adewara confirmed. "Ensign Rommel is helping Lord Commander Natas advance his own agenda by acting in his name. I just need to know what that agenda is so that we can understand it. This Ensign Rommel is a total fraud, leading a misguided people to their deaths for reasons beyond their own understanding. Like Lord Commander Natas, Rommel has been lying to his people to manipulate them into doing things to justify an utterly false cause."

"What can we do about our current situation?" Aamira asked. Talking about Rommel's motivations and heartless tactics would get them nowhere unless they had a plan to stop him.

Adewara shook his head. "Nothing. We must wait. Luckily, time is on our side. It seems Rommel knows now that one of the princesses of Sahael is here at the wall leading the forces. He's never faced anything like that. The fact that he sent a message at all shows how nervous he is. A loss here would look very bad for him in the eyes of Natas."

"That gives me the time I need to tell you all more about the Ensign, the Dyad in the bloodline that was created," Ryal said, chewing his loaf. "The Templars helped Ensign Rommel achieve his promise to Lord Commander Natas."

"Aren't the Templars religious zealots of the witan faith?" Yinká questioned.

"This was the time of the Templar's creation, yes," Ryal continued. "Ensign Rommel said to those he conquered that he was sent to save all Aardians from what they don't know. Taking it upon himself to 'educate' the people, he was able to ensure that his message, or more precisely Natas's message, was the only truth taught to the rising generations."

"It's easy to conquer people and force your teachings on them," Adewara said.

"Indeed," Ryal said.

"Tell me what teachings were forced on them," Aamira said.

"Natas was able to change the way they'd control those conquered," Ryal said. "It was pure genius. Lord Commander Natas made his son Damien a savior, a Messiah, that would take away all their sins, but only if the conquered witans accepted his form of religion."

"They were perverting Ishtar and Obatala's plan," Yomí said.

Ryal swallowed a bite of bread. "Exactly. Lie with a bit of truth, and as long as you're saying what the people want to hear, they will go along with it even if it means slaughtering their neighbors. After creating the Nauthian religion, Ensign Rommel was ordered by Lord Commander Natas to proselytize in the 'Arth Nations, and the States of 'Or."

"Ensign Rommel received his orders directly from the Trinity," Adewara said, nodding. "Those witan bloodlines had grown powerful by then. You must remember, there are very few of the old blood who can live for many centuries. Those of regular lifespan forget the lessons their ancestors learned. Natas counts on this to confuse and sow doubt. He can plant a false narrative like a weed that slowly grows over five generations until it is believed by almost all the people. Those of us who have lived for ten generations know the truth, but our voices are drowned out by men like Rommel and the poor fools he's seduced."

"Ensign Rommel has help, of course," Ryal agreed. "He instructed templar missionaries to learn the people's cultures, customs, strengths, and weaknesses. The Trinity created roads to help spread the Nauthian religion by visiting each village, city, nation, and state. The Templar missionaries preached the Nauthian doctrine throughout all Western Aarde and converted many to their cause. The witans in the States of 'Or, and the 'Arth Nations wanted to believe in their own gods, gods that looked like them and shared their lust for power. Natas was then able to create a system of witan supremacy.

"The witans that rejected their religion created tensions amongst the 'Arth Nations and the States of 'Or. The first rejections received the attention of Head Urban I, who helped create the divinity; a fabricated savior for all witans based on Damien in skin-changed witan form."

"Ensign Rommel was charged with spreading Lord Commander Natas's message, by any means necessary," Adewara said.

Ryal leaned against the battlements and gazed out on the ocean. "I have stood here many times over the past 200 years. My father for a century before that. I have seen generations fall into darkness, knowing that for a time, my father and I were also deceived by Lord Commander Natas. We were there when the demon sent out decrees to all western Aarde, to those who would soon be under witan rule. No one was allowed to question their ideas and thoughts. Natas said the Nauthian religion would accept every witan as Ishtar and Obatala accepted their own children. Ensign Rommel said that Head Urban I is the one who has direct contact with Ishtar and Obatala and the ability to receive revelation from both of them. A perversion of all goodness."

"Ensign Rommel ordered Lord Commander Natas to create a religious army of warrior monks known as the Templars," Adewara said.

"Interesting," Aamira admitted. So much history had taken place along the wall. Now she stood where all these things had transpired.

"The Templars," Adewara said, teeth grit. "It was a way to keep the people they converted trapped in the lie of a new way of life. Some of those converted became Templars themselves, representing the right and left arm of their religious savior, Damien, who was black himself, but they had no idea because of Natas's and Romell's teachings. Natas would appear to them in the form of a witan angel and proclaim his gospel. They had no idea the level of manipulation. They were to be seen as god's army. whatever they did was always done in Damien's name; not the son of Ishtar, but the son of Natas, a demon himself in all but flesh."

"Ensign Rommel believed his actions were justified by the truth with his involvement and conquest of the 'Arth Nations and the States of 'Or," Ryal said.

Yomí scratched his chin, obviously deep in thought. "So, if the witans have been deceived, couldn't we simply counteract that deception with the truth?"

"The Indoctrination process woke up something within all witans," Adewara replied. "A White Darkness of power and hate. The Templars preached a religious message centered around the claim that Damien was the one to save all his brothers and sisters from damnation. The Ennead were then used to enforce and spread the Nauthian religion."

"Not all witans have been consumed by hate and power," Ryal said quietly.

Eyes sharp as knives, Adewara stared at the wooly dreadlocked haired blond man. "I'm unconvinced. I believe the white darkness is being used as a means of communicating and receiving information from Lord Commander Natas. The Templars taught about Damien's nine Ennead Commanders and how Lord Commander Natas assumed control of nine legions in Damien's name. The other three Commander's consisted of Lord Commander Natas's right and left-hand General Commander Norg, and Vice Commander Uré. They were to prepare the way for Natas's four Generals."

Aamira had heard enough. Below them, Narsan ships had now tied together less than a thousand yards from the main gate. If Rommel's plan was true, he would soon send gliders to ride the wind and drop nitrate bombs from above. The bombs would do nothing to the wall itself, but the casualties they would cause could be devastating.

"All this history is fine," Aamira said, taking the last loaf of bread from Adewara's basket. "But I need history that will help us survive the next 24 hours. Ryal, you know Rommel's tactics. What can we expect?"

Running his hands through his blond locked hair, Ryal blew out a deep breath. "I'm betting he uses similar tactics to when he systematically took control of the States of 'Or, who resisted the Templars from a religious standpoint."

"What did he do?" Yinká asked.

"The States of 'Or were surrounded by water on every side that provided proper protection. They then had stone walls higher than even the Nibiru Wall on which we stand. Ensign Rommel had men climb up the mountain rock structure much like he tried two days ago here. It didn't work. So instead, Ensign Rommel's seals created caves within the rock structure. Ensign Rommel spent years working on a way to forcibly submit the States of 'Or to the

Nauthian religion until his men inched closer to the city getting within two miles. An Orichalcum plate was discovered beneath the surface of States of 'Or that covered the circumference of the continent, preventing Rommel and his army from invading those states from within."

"So, you're saying he's willing to wait years, slowly undermining our position?" Aamira asked.

Ryal nodded. "You are still in what would be considered your first lifetime, Empress. Eventually you will understand that even ten years to some of us is considered a very short amount of time."

"And if we're stuck here unable to retreat," Adewara added, "then the redemption of Sahael will simply be pushed off by that amount of time. Either way, Natas claims a victory."

"What happened after they found the Orichalcum cover?" Yomí asked.

"The Orichalcum plate prevented Ensign Rommel from being able to dig through the structure," Ryal described. "After thirty days, Ensign Rommel devised a plan that would get him and his men into the city."

"How?" Aamira asked.

"Love," Ryal said.

"What do you mean?"

"Ensign Rommel had a child with a woman who lived in the States of 'Or." Ryal said. "During the Narsan's years on the mountain trying to gain entry, they developed relationships with traders. Rommel seduced one of the women and impregnated her. There's a location in Blackland Island in Dark City that carries people on airships to the states of 'Or. The Narsans have special passes that allow entry, but Rommel wasn't permitted entry because he didn't possess a State pass. To this day, such passes are issued only to state citizens the moment they're born. After the birth of his child, whose mother was a full citizen, Ensign Rommel met back up with his mistress and used the new child's pass to gain entry to the city."

"He manipulated a lonely woman and that's how he got into 'Or?" Aamira asked, more disgusted with the man than she had been before.

"According to reports," Ryal continued, "the woman loved him deeply. Whether he had any affection for her is unknown. In any case, Rommel learned the hidden entrances and passwords and soon breached the city with his forces. They set fire to everything. After several days of fighting, Ensign Rommel's troops started targeting the children. With that action, the states quickly gave up, and as a result, those that fought against Ensign Rommel's seals were executed."

In her mind, Aamira could imagine the devastation Rommel had unleashed. Now he stood on one of those ships below her, planning how to retake the wall. Did the Ensign know they had less than 200 people holding the castle? Would he strike quickly or try to starve them out? Would he find some sad Rysallian woman outside the wall one day and make her fall in love with him? She wished the bastard stood in front of her now so she could manifest one of her blades and castrate him with it.

"What happened to his child?" Yomí asked quietly.

Ryal shrugged. "I don't know. What I do know is that Ensign Rommel is a man who is intelligent, cunning, and ruthless. He takes no chances in what he does. His spies are patient and devious. They were able to enter our fortress during our own last stand and overcome us from within. Ensign Rommel will find any weakness you have and use it against you, forcing you to fail in the end."

"His spies are that good?" Aamira asked.

"They are."

"So, our weaknesses within this castle will be exposed," Adewara said, forehead furrowed.

"What do we do?" Yinká asked.

Looking out on the ocean to the east, Aamira came to a decision. The Rysallians were strong and skilled in battle, but no matter what, Rommel would eventually beat them. It could take a week, or a year, depending on a lot of factors. She and her forces had taken the wall to facilitate their escape, and now it would be their tomb unless they abandoned it.

"We're leaving," Aamira stated finally.

"What?" Ryal asked, seemingly taken aback.

"We can fight and die, or we can leave. It's that simple. The Nibiru wall is not a part of your heritage, but it's just a wall as far as I'm concerned. Natas can have it back. We need to head to Sahael. We need to find the rest of my family, which means we need to sail toward Inheritance. That's the choice I'm making. You can choose the same or stay here."

A smile filled Adewara's face. "I think that is an excellent plan."

"I don't think my father will accept that," Ryal said, eyes blinking rapidly.

"Does he seek forgiveness?" Aamira asked.

"He does."

"Does he want to help in the redemption of Sahael and the return of the bloodlines?"

"He does."

"Would he rather his people be welcomed into Ishtar and

Obatala's sacred land or die defending a wall?"

Ryal looked at his feet.

Aamira turned and walked to the far side of the wall, looking into Western Aarde. A line of ships filled the small city a few miles away as merchants waited to be let through the gates.

"Anyone who wants to join us needs to be ready by sundown," she said while staring down at the ships. "We escape under cover of darkness and then steal one of those ships. If we move quickly, we can be off the wall before anyone is aware, down to the town within an hour, and sail on a stolen vessel within two hours of that. By the middle of the second watch, we should be on the waves toward Inheritance."

"I can start spreading the word," Adewara offered.

Aamira turned and nodded toward her sons. "I want a message sent to Admiral Rommel. Tell him tomorrow morning at first light I will meet with him in person to discuss terms. Tell him I will sail in a small boat and meet him on his command ship."

Yomí grinned broadly. "He'll think you're coming to parlay, so he won't attack tonight just in case you have something better to offer him."

"Exactly," Aamira said. "By the time he realizes we've escaped and where we went, we'll be a full day ahead of him. Plus, he'll have no idea where we're going, so the advantage falls to us. Spread the word. Anyone who stays behind is on their own."

CHAPTER IV
INHERITANCE ISLAND

Aarde, Western Aarde, Inheritance

No one stayed behind.

As soon as darkness fell, Aamira, her sons, Adewara, and the remaining Rysallians, abandoned the Nibiru Wall through the sewers and exited the culverts into Western Aarde. Ryland had been hesitant to leave the lands of his first inheritance but understood their plight better than anyone. His repentant spirit and humility influenced his people, who looked to Aamira as a savior of sorts. They would follow her anywhere.

Stealing a ship had been easy, as most of the sailors were in the brothels and inns of the town, leaving only a handful of guards sleeping onboard most of the ships. Knowing the different types of merchant vessels, Ryland chose a large craft named *Dar Linkonte*, Vannadale slang for 'Nigger Chains.'

A slave ship.

The vessel was empty of slaves now of course, having dropped its cargo along the western coasts before heading back to the Vannadale colonies for a fresh batch of captives.

Aamira and her sons had entered the ship before midnight, killing all five sailors aboard and throwing their bodies into the ocean. The Rysallians had boarded after that, and within an hour, they had pulled away from the docks and set their sails west toward Inheritance.

Three weeks had passed. Mild weather accompanied the journey, save for a few stormy days of lightning and hail. Efforts had been made to clean the slave quarters and remove any evidence of the disgusting practice. Yomí and Yinká had even hung themselves over the side of the ship with ropes so they could remove the large wooden placards that read *Dar Linkonte*. One of the Rysallian women, a woodworker by trade, had removed the letters and carved new ones with axes she found onboard. The placards now read: *Linkonte Quebrad*, Vannadale slang for 'Broken Chains.'

According to Adewara, they would be arriving in his homeland any day.

A horn blast woke Aamira at first light. She rolled from her bed in the captain's quarters and stepped onto the deck bleary eyed.

"What is it?" she shouted to one of the Rysallian sailors manning the wheel.

"Adewara has spotted land, my empress," the man replied.

"It looks as if we've arrived," Adewara cried from the upper deck while leaning over the railing to look down on Aamira. "We need to sail more toward the south. I can see through my spyglass that a ship is anchored in a bay that direction."

"What ship?" Aamira asked, an expectant squeak to her voice.

Adewara simply smiled.

As they sailed closer to the island of Inheritance, Aamira saw only what looked like black barren ground with no green to speak of. The closer they sailed to the island, the bleaker the area appeared. Nothing could live here. No wonder Natas had left the island alone.

By midday, the *Linkonte Quebrad* anchored beside the large ship Aamira and her family had taken from Timbuktu. Admiral Abdul waved from the deck, smiling broadly.

"My Empress!" the admiral shouted. "We hoped you would find us sooner as opposed to later. I see you stole a ship that is not as nice as the one we got from Timbuktu."

"It's not," Aamira laughed. "We at least cleaned up where the slaves were kept. This ship will never transport another slave again. Where are my sons and husband?"

Abdul pointed toward the coastline. "They've been exploring every day to see if they can find anything. You'll find them on shore."

Aamira saw several lifeboats on a black sand beach not far away. With only one lifeboat on the slave vessel, only Aamira, her sons, Adewara, and Ryal left the ship. Before they reached the beach, Aamira saw her husband and two other sons walk out from behind an outcropping of rock, smiling and waving to the new arrivals.

Unable to contain himself, Abioye ran into the water and swam toward the small boat. Aamira laughed and jumped into the waves toward her husband. They kissed in the salty water and smiled at each other without speaking. How their relationship had flourished after so many years of emotional estrangement. Aamira loved this man, and he loved her. She would never go back to those days when they barely spoke, let alone touched and pleasured each other.

They were together again.

I knew I wouldn't have to wait too long to see you again, Abioye said telepathically to his wife.

And I knew you would wait for me, Aamira smiled back.

Within a few minutes, the boat pulled up on the sand and Aamira's sons hugged each other and joked about how surprised they were that the other group had survived at all without the more skilled brothers to save them.

Once the reunion was finished, Yinká kicked at the black sand and gazed out on the lifeless land all around them. "Where are we? This can't be where your people are, Adewara."

"We are in Inheritance," Adewara said as he pulled on the rope to make sure the lifeboat was completely out of the water. "This is a land full of history and turmoil. We are where my people have remained hidden since the fall of Sahael. We came here to preserve the knowledge and history of the Chosen order. Most of the surface is semi-smooth and rocky. You won't need to walk far before you encounter skeletons, old weapons, and animal carcasses. This is a land of death…and of life, since it has sheltered my people for almost 50 years."

"You guys know your way around?" Yomí asked his brothers.

"We don't," Yemí replied. "Every day we wander around looking for any life before returning to the ship to eat and sleep. We haven't found anything."

Adewara started walking up the charred rocks inland. "Follow me. I know the way."

As the Educator had mentioned, it didn't take them long to come upon old bones of men and beasts scattered here and there. Ash covered everything.

"**We** are approaching the entrance into Inheritance," Adewara said as they walked. "This has been a safe haven for my people, who are a part of the ancient order of bloodlines. It was all part of Solomon's plan to keep us away from each other; though it's for reasons my people and I have yet to understand."

"How long have you and your people lived below the surface of Inheritance?" Abioye asked with sweat dripping down his forehead.

"My people have lived secretly under the surface of Inheritance, residing two miles deep."

"How is that possible?" Aamira asked. The thought of living underground for a few days, let alone decades, made her feel claustrophobic even walking through the flat expanse under the hot sun.

"Inheritance was meant as a sanctuary," Adewara explained as he climbed over a boulder. "Massive crystals make up the ceiling of the underground expanse. These crystals capture the energy of the sun from the surface of Aarde and shine it below. Because of this, everything that would grow above ground grows beneath the surface as well, including crops and plants. We even have animals and running streams, small lakes teeming with fish, and many other things as if they were living above ground. We're getting close, so pay attention."

The Royal family, Adewara and Ryal arrived at a large, ten-foot diameter circular door beneath an outcropping of charred rock. The door appeared to be orichalcum and had a prominent Marula Tree symbol in the center, with icons representing the bloodlines of the first and the second gathering.

"How do we get inside?" Yinká asked.

Adewara's eyes began to glow. The entrance suddenly became transparent, allowing The Royal family, Adewara and Ryal entry below the surface of Inheritance. A large cave upended up before them, with glowing crystals along the walls. The sound of water roared in the darkness ahead.

"We'll need to ride the river for a while. There should be some log boats up here." Adewara pointed to their left where four boats were tied to a rock. They were long and thin, holding six people apiece. "We will move directly into an opening with a large eddy. It will suck our log boat into the underground Heritance River that will lead us to lake Tance."

The group climbed into two different boats, with Aamira, Adewara, Abioye, and Ryal in one, and the four boys in the other. The river pulled them along swiftly, with clumps of crystals casting light on the underground river at reliable intervals.

"How's all of this possible?" Yomí asked.

"The ancients had knowledge and skill that has been lost, unfortunately," Adewara said as the river sped up. "There's a sinkhole that will open, activated by my people on the other side when the signs of entry are accepted. The symbols must be presented in a specific order."

"What happens if the sigils are presented incorrectly?" Yekú asked, practically shouting as the roar from the water increased.

"The eddy won't allow us through. It will consume us, crushing our boat."

"Then we need to make sure you get this right." Abioye said.

The river twisted to the right and they entered a large chasm with stalactites hanging from the ceiling 50 feet above. The water swirled and dropped toward a whirlpool of devastating fury.

"It's the eddy!" Aamira cried.

"Hold on!" Abioye shouted.

Adewara stood up in the boat as they circled the center of the whirlpool again and again. He raised his arms above his head, performing the necessary signals with his hands and fingers. Just as predicted, when they approached the sinkhole, it opened, and they were all engulfed and emerged in Inheritance.

Water sprayed in Aamira's face. It felt for a second as if the world had dropped out from beneath them. They splashed and swirled before the river once again pointed them forward. Darkness consumed them until light grew in front of them like the end of a lonely tunnel.

"Where are we?" Aamira asked as they exited the tunnel into a massive cave filled with sunlight. Trees lined the banks of the river, which opened onto a tranquil lake filled with fishing boats. Aamira could tell they weren't outside, but the warmth from the light above tickled her skin. Fragrances of flowers and moist air filled her nostrils.

"This is Tance Lake," Adewara replied with a smile. "We need to dock the log boat and wait to be escorted from the docks and brought to the inner sanctum. According to custom, we will then be escorted into Centropolis, where my people, the Lysinnians, have lived for many years in isolation. When you arrive, you will see that there is no hierarchy amongst my people; we are treated as one and the same."

Fishermen on nearby boats waved and called to Adewara with bright smiles. He would call back to them by name, a laughter in his voice Aamira had never heard before.

The boat pulled into the docks where a crowd had formed. Everyone seemed excited by the visitors, but more focused on Adewara.

"You have returned!" an old man with a gray beard yelled

to Adewara as a rope was thrown to Abioye to help bring the boat closer to the dock.

"I have, Philemon!" Adewara cried. "Where are they? Do they know I'm here?"

Philemon reached toward Adewara as the boat drew near and pulled the Educator onto the dock and into a powerful hug.

"The crystals vibrated with the entry warning when you passed through the eddy," Philemon said. The first fishermen saw you on the river and immediately sent word here. They should be close by now, but---"

"Father!" a woman shouted as she ran along the wooden docks. She was followed by three other women, all with long hair varying in length, their eyes the color of Amethyst. All four of them had fine braided hair to the middle of their backs and stood six feet five inches tall. Three of the beautiful women had roasted chestnut skin, while the fourth was a beautiful albino woman with pale features and braids.

"My daughter!" Adewara cried, face shining with joy. He ran forward and hugged each of them as they all cried together.

Aamira stepped out of the boat with her family and Ryal. The Lysinnian people looked at Ryal curiously and with trepidation. Aamira assumed there had never been a witan here before.

"Adewara has daughters?" Yomí asked Aamira.

"Why didn't he ever tell us?" Yinká questioned, face somewhat sad, as if he hadn't been privy to very important information.

Abioye placed his hand on his son's shoulder. "Educators are incredibly private. They share only what they need to share. You know this."

"Yeah," Yekú shrugged. "They don't share knowledge unless you're ready to ask the right questions, but this is different. He's been our mentor our entire lives. You'd think he would have shared something like this."

"Only a month ago in Timbuktu I learned that Adewara is married," Aamira admitted. "He only told me because I could see the emotion on his face when talking about the Educator that is with my cousin Oadira. Her name is Lyshyla."

Yemí waved his hand angrily at the hugging family and walked off. Aamira didn't know what to say. The only thing she could do would be to let her sons feel their sadness at not having been deemed important enough to know even the basic life details of their teacher and guide.

"Emperor and Empress," Adewara said as he led his daughters toward Aamira and Abioye. "May I present my four daughters, Lilly, Leesha, Lyla, and Lanae. They will lead us to Centropolis where we will eat and rest. There is a lot that needs to be discussed and more that needs to be done. We must gather our people quickly; we must speak now!"

"What's happening, Father?" one of his daughters asked.

"The Signs of times are upon us, Lanae" Adewara replied. "The precursor to the gathering has been set in motion. Make the announcement to all Lysinnians that live under this subterranean continent. Time is of the essence."

Lanae nodded and stepped towards Aamira. "I admire your emerald eyes and all that you've accomplished to get here. I am Lanae, youngest daughter of Educators Adewara and Lyshyla, spokesperson for our clan in my father and mother's absence."

"I am Aamira, Empress Adesola, and this is my husband, Abioye, Emperor Adesola. My sons are Yomí, Yemí, Yekú, and Yinká, though Yemí has…stepped away for a moment." She looked at Adewara as she spoke the last sentence. Adewara blinked and looked around for Yemí. He glanced at the other princes, whose faces were masks of disappointment.

"I'm sure Yemí just needed to settle his stomach after the rush of the river," Adewara said unconvincingly.

"I doubt it," Yekú replied as he walked past Adewara without looking at him.

Lanae stepped forward again as if sensing the tension. "I see the glow of a heart stone beneath your tunic, Empress. Is that Inkalamu's Heart around your neck?"

"It is," Aamira said, noticing for the first time that the stone had begun to glow when they entered the underground realm. "We passed through trials to get it, knowing it would be needed in our people's redemption."

"Follow me," Lanae said. "My sisters and I will lead you toward a place of rest and comfort."

The Royal family, Adewara, and Ryal followed Lanae along a cobblestone path through a lush forest. Fruit trees grew everywhere with birds singing in their branches. The air smelled clean and fresh despite the fact that they were deep underground. People working in the fields would stop their labor and wave happily at the passing crowd. Many of the fishermen followed along after the royal family, singing and praising Ishtar.

"This is an impressive place," Abioye said as they walked past a cow munching on some grass.

"It certainly is," Lanae replied as she strode beside her sisters. "Right now, we're making our way to Nibiru Palace, which is surrounded by the seven cities of Iru, a place that was once home to the Nibiru people before they disappeared."

After a half hour of walking, the group entered a city of

stone and crystal. Merchants and families stopped and whispered at the sight of the gathering. Buildings seemed to sparkle in the light and cast rainbows of color all around.

"Are those prisms?" Yinká asked as a cascade of color shone across his face.

"They are indeed," Lanae answered. "Much of the foundation of the city is crystalline. Think of the cavern as one massive geode. We are blessed to have this land as our sanctuary."

They came to a large palace in the center of the city with pillars made of single shafts of crystal. People gathered around, rejoicing as they learned this was indeed the emperor and empress of the Yoruban bloodline.

Lanae and her sisters led the royal family to rooms on the ground floor. Food was brought in, and Aamira was able to bathe in fresh water for the first time in weeks. She and Abioye made love and enjoyed the sounds of the city echoing through the open veranda door.

"I missed you," Abioye said as he snuggled in bed beside his wife.

"I missed you too. How many people do you think are down here?"

"No idea. It doesn't sound like anyone lives in the surrounding cities from what Lanae said, but there are a lot living here, that's for sure. Tens of thousands at least."

After getting dressed, the couple sat on the veranda next to a group of trees. A lizard scurried across a rock near her feet. Looking up at the cave roof, she watched as the crystals slowly changed colors to red and purple, as if the sun was setting.

A knock at the door pulled Aamira's attention from the strange view overhead. Her sons entered the apartment informing their parents Adewara had summoned all of them, including Ryal. The family made their way upstairs to the Nibiru council room where a rectangular table sat beside Nephrophida's interactive map on the wall behind. Lanae, Lilly, Leesha, Adewara, and Ryal were already sitting around the table. Seven other individuals lined the table as well, four men and three women, all dressed in robes that made Aamira think they were of some importance among the people of Inheritance.

"Please, sit, royal family of the Yoruban line," Lanae said, motioning for them to join the others. "Joining us here are the leaders of the seven Iru cities. This is our council, and we will discuss your arrival and how that affects our people and Aarde itself."

"We were surprised to be summoned so soon," Abioye said as he sat down in a wooden chair. "We thought we would reconvene tomorrow."

"This Nibiru stronghold has housed our bloodline long enough," Adewara said. "This place was built for them by Ishtar and Obatala to protect them from all of those who seek to see them dead and have control of the Nibiru wall."

"They didn't do a great job," Yekú said, face calm but obviously unhappy. "The Nibiru Wall has been under Natas's control for over a century."

"Are the Nibiru even alive?" Yinká asked.

"Yes," Lanae replied.

"Then where are they?" Yinká questioned.

"They are deep behind their inactive gates beyond Centropolis," she answered. "Our people were permitted to dwell within Centropolis until the scattering of Sahael was finished. The scattering is now a gathering that needs to take place, but forces are preventing it from taking root."

"Yes, Daughter," Adewara said. "During the fall of Sahael, the ancient bloodlines were unable to make it to the Nairohenge gates within the city. As a result, they were enslaved, transported to the provinces to be worked to death, and systematically exterminated. It is rumored that those of Inheritance that were selected and enslaved were sent to Western Aarde in ships for reasons we don't understand. We are continually looking for answers to the questions we don't have. To find them, we must get you and your family back to Sahael."

"Interesting that you would have unanswered questions," Yekú said. "All of you are Educators, I would assume. It seems like leaving things out is your only way of living. It must be frustrating to find yourself as the one without answers."

"Quiet, Yekú," Abioye interrupted. "Now is not the time."

"I disagree," Aamira said, folding her arms. She could see her sons' pain at having been left out of such an important part of the life of a man they respected dearly. They deserved to know why. *She* deserved to know why. "Educators love answering questions when the time is right, and I would have my questions answered. How come you never told us you had daughters, Adewara?"

"It was not important at the time," Adewara replied. "All that was important was helping you and your family get to Sahael. I knew my daughters were always safe; the signs were my peace. In addition to that, you never asked."

A snort blew from Yomí's nose. "Yeah, it's our fault we never knew. Thanks for making it clear how stupid and incompetent we are."

"Yomí," Adewara began. "That is not what---"

"Not what you meant?" Yekú interrupted. "No, tell my brother what you meant. That we were never important enough to you to share anything like that? How about you're nothing but a machine that we can't trust? That one seems more like the truth."

"Stop it, boys," Abioye urged as he held his hand up.

Yemí sat forward and pointed at Adewara. "You're the only Educator we've ever met. You taught us and fought beside us, and we thought we knew you. But it turns out that we never really knew you at all. Do you understand how that damages whatever relationship we thought we had with you? We shared our hopes and dreams with you, and you couldn't even tell us you had a family. That hurts incredibly bad. Are you even capable of understanding it? This isn't about whether you have daughters or a wife or a dog or a bad cough. This is about the fact that after 30 years, we don't know you at all. That hurts. I think I speak for my brothers when I say, keep doing your Educator thing and making all of us feel stupid because we didn't ask the right question at the right time with the exact right words. Keep doing it. Just don't expect us to trust you ever again. As far as I'm concerned, you're a paid guide. Nothing more."

The chair squeaked as Yemí sat back. Adewara looked down at the table in silence. Aamira thought about opening her mouth and saying something, but felt the silence needed to weigh on Adewara. He was always so focused on his mission that he forgot the human cost of his indifference. He had broken the trust of her sons, and of her. Regaining it would be a difficult effort, and she doubted Adewara would even try. Such was the way of the Educator. Damn them all.

Lanae coughed "Restoring the ancient bloodlines takes precedence over the needs of every single Lysinnian and Egyptian," she said as if trying to change the subject. "We're of the same bloodline that was merged years ago and were selected to remain here until the time to depart came upon us. My Empress, my Emperor, there is much more that needs to be done. We're at the forefront of something unprecedented that is taking place. The Nabtahenge gates have emerged from the center of the great hall inside Nibiru palace.”

“The Nairohenge Gates are operational here?” Abioye asked.

“We still can’t use them to travel anywhere in Aarde until the Navigators and Medjay Gate guardians have been found,” Adewara said quietly. “However, we can use them to travel anywhere in Inheritance. That is how the leaders of the seven cities were able to arrive so quickly.”

“My father, Adewara, my sisters and I have been on a mission to help get the Yoruban Bloodline to Sahael,” Lanae said.

“And we are to believe these are the true bloodline?” one of the city leaders asked with a gravelly voice. “We have been deceived before.”

“Prove it to us,” another Iru councilman said.

“Fine,” Aamira said. She looked at her sons as her eyes glowed green. The princes did the same. The power emanated from their irises, reflecting on the smooth table.

“More is required,” a woman on the Iru council replied. “Show us your ancient power.”

“What more is required?” Aamira asked. “Adewara can vouch for us. We lived in Neros’s Realm for 16 years. Before that, he was with us in the sand lands of IFF serving Abioye’s father until my arrival.”

“Words do not suffice,” the first city leader spoke again. “Death is the metric.”

“What’s going on?” Yinká asked Adewara, who stared forward, stone-faced without reply.

“Lanae,” Adewara said finally, “order the guards to

proceed.”

Lanae clapped her hands and in response, twelve Egyptian Knights from the twelve pyramids of Egypt stepped into the council room from the far entryway.

“Guards,” Lanae shouted. “Kill these royal princes in the name of the Lysinnian people.”

“What is the meaning of this?” Aamira shouted, standing up.

“The Sacred proving,” Adewara said. “There is no intervening. Your four sons have a sacred responsibility of fighting to the death. They are to use their gifts, their Abilities, Artes, and Powers, to defeat the greatest warriors in our realm.”

“You bastard,” Yekú spat at Adewara. “They won’t beat us! These men will die just so you can prove…what?! This is stupid!”

Even so, the guards rushed forward, pulling their swords. Yekú, already standing, formed a blade of green light in his right hand and jumped backwards towards two of the soldiers. He sliced before they realized he had moved, losing their heads in the process. A sword slammed against the table as another knight tried to kill Yekú, but the prince simply strafed and plunged his blade into the sternum of the man and twisted mercilessly.

The urge to stand filled Aamira’s veins, but she looked at Adewara and saw the pain in his face. Whatever her sons thought of the Educator, he only wanted their safety and happiness. She needed to trust Adewara despite her own frustrations. Ishtar’s ways were not her ways, and Adewara knew the old gods like few people on Aarde.

Yemí followed his brother’s lead by conjuring Egyptian daggers and tossing them at three of the advancing guards. The blades cut through their armor like nothing and pierced the hearts of the Egyptian Knights.

Yomí jumped high into the air, using his powers of Terrakinesis to create holes in the floor. The guards stepped into these surprise traps and fell forward, allowing Yomí to slice off three of their heads simultaneously.

The three remaining Egyptian Knights lined themselves up shoulder to shoulders and approached Yinká. Suddenly, a tattoo appeared on Yinká's neck, glowing bright green. He opened his mouth and shouted in their direction. The sound was ear-shattering. Aamira covered her ears, as did everyone else in the room. Zambian colored waves shot from Yinká's mouth, disintegrated the Egyptian Knights into nothing but ash. Aamira stared as pieces of what seconds before had been strapping warriors, floated on the air like lint. Tears came to Yinká's eyes as he looked to his mother for answers.

"What was that?" Yemí shouted. "You killed them with a word!"

"I didn't mean to!" Yinká said, breathing deeply and leaning against the table. "I wanted them to stop. That's all. I swear!"

"It is your Gift of Shout," Adewara said, emotionless. "Given to you by Ikegwuru after you rescued her children."

"I remember," Yinká gasped. "I didn't know it would…how can I…?"

The council all clapped their hands in unison.

"Proof has been given," the lead councilman stated. "The death of these warriors is a testimony to the truthfulness of the sacred bloodline."

"This is madness!" Yekú shouted.

"This is the Sign of the Times!" Adewara shouted back,

standing and slamming his hands against the table. Saliva flew from his lips. "Death is following you! Natas will have your heads on the prow of his ship if he can. Don't you understand what's at stake? Don't you understand anything I've taught you?!"

The princes stood together, glaring at Adewara. For a moment, Aamira was afraid they would jump across the table and kill their mentor.

"We need to explain to you how Sahael was destroyed," Lanae said.

Abioye rubbed his forehead. "We know how Sahael was destroyed."

"Do you know what Sahael is and what Sahael represents?" Lanae asked. She motioned for the princes to sit once more.

"We'll stand, thank you," Yomí said for all four of them.

"As you wish," Lanae continued. "Sahael used to be a haven for the twelve bloodlines in Sahael. Sahaelians used the Nabtahenge gates to travel in and out of Timbuktu, to Sahael, and then back to Inheritance. The bloodlines who were traveling to Sahael were not aware of the invasion of Sahael."

"Due to the confusion, the chosen order of the bloodlines was scattered all over Aarde to avoid being enslaved by the Narsans," Adewara said.

"The bloodlines never had the opportunity to make it back to Inheritance," Lanae said, making eye contact with the royal family. "When the tribes chose to come down from Ishtar's and Obatala's presence, Inheritance became a place where the bloodlines could rest. However, an enormous disagreement had taken place in Inheritance. As a result, it became a battleground. The Rysallians were coerced into thinking that the other bloodlines conspired to keep all the power that Ishtar and Obatala had given them and that it was taken away. The other eleven bloodlines were told that the other tribes knew the Rysallian bloodline would have their power to use it to enslave them. The Rysallians felt this way primarily because half of the Rysallian bloodline was stained with witan blood which was different from the other eleven and a half bloodlines."

Adewara nodded. "Damien penetrated the witan minds of the Rysallians, explaining to them that they were different. Damien said that they would be treated differently due to the color of their witan skin. Damien convinced them that they were better than the ancients and superior in every way. The doctrine permeated the minds of the witan Rysallians, indoctrinating them, warping their sense of reality and distorting their way of thinking."

"**We** have Rysallians with us," Aamira interrupted. "Both of black skin and witan. They fight by our side and have sought forgiveness for their sins."

"I don't doubt it," Lanae said.

Ryal stood and bowed. "My father, myself, and what remains of my people, less than 200 strong, have cast off the lies of Natas and wish to serve our brother bloodlines."

"We understand," Lanae said. "Even so, every witan Rysallian started to believe that Aarde was for them, and they were destined to conquer it to save it. Damien preached this as he indoctrinated them with knowledge of his creed, to conquer Aarde in his name. The witan Rysallians chose to leave, deciding to go to Narsa and continue to learn from Damien, awaiting their Lord Commander with the understanding he would have a plan to save all Aardians."

"We know the plan," Abioye said. "He wants to prove that his plan to bring everyone back to Ishtar and Obatala's presence is superior to their plan."

"That is the consequence of the plan," one of the council

women replied. "But that is not the plan."

"Then what is the plan?" Aamira asked, suddenly feeling very tired. She realized for the first time that she was seated at a table surrounded by Educators. Merely being in the room was exhausting.

"We don't know," Lanae answered. "This is another reason why you and your family must get to Sahael. Once there, the bloodlines can combine all that they know to put all the pieces together. Only then can we combat Natas before he plunges Aarde into darkness. It will be like the days when the Ukáváál destroyed Kolob and sent the Kemites into the universe."

"Exactly," Adewara continued. "Ishtar and Obatala sent Solomon, the protector of Aarde, down to this realm many years before the bloodlines were sent here. Solomon, the protector of Aarde helped the Nibiru build the Nibiru wall, splitting Aarde into Western Aarde and Eastern Aarde. He did many things under Ishtar and Obatala's guidance to help their children on this plane of existence. The gods also sent the Watchers to assist the Alkebulan people. Solomon taught the Watchers how to care for and serve the Alkebulan people; to help the Ancient bloodlines thrive. The Watchers were able to travel through the Nairohenge gates. This provoked the witan Rysallians, who were intentionally left out of the loop for the safety of the other bloodlines."

Lanae stood at the front of the table and leaned forward. "The Rysallians were not made aware of the subterranean home under Inheritance. The witan half then traveled and took over the T.I.M. Lands. The Black Rysallians traveled to the abandoned 'Afe lands. These are the direct family of the witan Ryal whom you brought with you to our home."

"Ryal and his father Ryland are honorable," Aamira stated.

"We wish for reconciliation," Ryal agreed.

"The Educators recorded your history, Ryal of the witan Rysallians" the lead Iru councilman said. "These witans justified the slaughter of their kin by claiming they were saving Aarde. The weaker continents were left to defend themselves and were closely monitored by the Narsans. When the Narsans took lands, they were able to build up resources for their own gain."

"Those who believe in Natas's vision believe he is what's best for Aarde," Lanae said. "That includes the witan Rysallians."

"Not all of them," Yemí replied angrily.

"Yes, all of them," an old councilwoman said, staring at Ryal. "The converts of the Nauthian gospel were taught about death. These converts discovered that death could save them by allowing Damien to take away their right of choice and submit to his control after death,"

"These new Nauthian converts thought it best to systematically take control of the western nations aligning themselves with the trinity," Lanae agreed. "They were fighting for control of the D.I.M. Lands, as an agreement was struck to mingle bloodlines, bringing the witan Rysallians into the fold of the T.I.M. to help fight the D.I.M. Death and chaos followed. The fall of Sahael was predicated first on these actions. The Narsans and Rysallians are one in the same."

"All of this happened because of the stupidity of one bloodline being manipulated!" another councilman said, smacking his hand against the table.

Ryal dropped his head and stared at his hands.

"Because of them, Nightfall very well may consume all of Aarde, even if you and your kin are able to redeem Sahael," Lanae said.

"What is Nightfall?" Yekú asked.

"No one truly knows," Adewara said, gripping his hands together. "We will know when Nightfall arrives by the long day of gray will proceed the permanently blackening of the skies."

"This is all new to me," Abioye said.

"Lord Commander Natas will be leading an army of his brothers and sisters through the talents and gifts secured from within the Rysallian bloodline," Adewara added. "Natas will use their talents, gifts, and abilities to help him conquer those who choose not to follow his religion and way of life."

Lanae pointed at Ryal. "Your people helped cause all the pain now felt by black people everywhere in Aarde. You yourself followed Natas for a time, did you not?"

Looking up, tears formed in Ryal's eyes. "I am filled with guilt and remorse. I want nothing more than to make amends for the actions and transgressions of myself and my people."

Now it was Aamira's turn to stand. She looked from one council member to the next. "I am a queen of the Yoruban bloodline, a Black Madonna, and Empress of Neros's Realm. Is there anyone here who would question my judgement?"

No one spoke.

"Good. I trust Ryal and his father Ryland, and all the witan and black people who are with them now from the Rysallian line. We know Rysallian blood is needed in the redemption of Sahael, so I say we will trust these our brothers and let them come with us to the dead lands. If Ishtar and Obatala deem them unworthy, they may make their will known at that time or show their displeasure with me directly. Are there any of you who would challenge this?"

Again, no one spoke.

Lanae nodded to her father, who motioned for her to continue. "Very good. It is decided then. Despite our concerns,

Empress Adesola and her family will travel to Sahael with the Rysallians joining them. For now, we welcome you officially to Inheritance. Rest, enjoy some peace and sustenance. We look forward to recording your histories and adding them to the records here, and eventually in Timbuktu as well. We apologize for how things unfolded in this council, but such are the Signs of the Times. If you would like to join us, we will have the evening meal under the crystal sky in the courtyard."

As they walked out, Aamira stepped over one of the bodies of the Egyptian Knights. His head was missing. She grimaced. What she imagined her family would experience here and what they had so far experienced were quite different from each other. Educators were rigid as a rule, but being in a place full of them was far more dangerous than she expected.

Despite her love and appreciation for Adewara, Aamira had to admit that he was every bit as extreme as the Narsans, only he fought for them instead of Natas. Now surrounded by Educators, she saw for the first time how terrible they could be while in pursuit of their goals. If she or her sons decided to stand against them for any reason, the Educators would not hesitate to kill them.

That thought clawed at her brain as she smiled and laughed over dinner.

CHAPTER V
THE SIGNS OF THE TIMES

Aarde, Inheritance, Centropolis

Over the next several weeks, the Royal family prepared to find a way to get back into Sahael. They spent time talking with the leaders of the cities, all of which were Educators. They shared their records and coded manuscripts.

One afternoon while eating lunch in the palace courtyard under a canopy, Adewara approached Aamira and Abioye. He held a large leather book. The air was humid and moist, sprinkling droplets of water occasionally like rain.

"The weather here is strange," Aamira said as Adewara wiped moisture from his forehead.

"It doesn't rain," Adewara said, placing the book on the table. "But these thick mists come in from the lakes when the temperatures are right, leaving behind quite a bit of water on everything. The plants like it, even if my books don't."

Abioye chuckled. "Well, I've never seen you walk into a room carrying a book without needing to share some kernel of information with us, so what do you have?"

"It says here the Ancient Kemite supreme leaders attached catastrophic events to the signs of the times," Adewara said. He sat down at the table between the couple and grabbed a handful of nuts as he talked. "The Kings and Queen of Khartoum Palace summoned Solomon the Protector of Aarde to restore the sight of the four princesses born blind from the four Watchers realms. This was how they were able to unite the realms as one."

"We're eating lunch, Adewara," Abioye said. "Can't this wait?"

"Not if we want to make it to Sahael before the end of the age," Adewara replied, munching some of the nuts. "Kaimana and Kainoa met with Solomon the protector of Aarde in the ancient city of Katunkumene in Andalusia. Solomon explained to the supreme leaders of the Kemites that the four baby princesses would be the Black Madonnas of their respective bloodlines. Solomon said the Black Madonnas were the only ones who could save Aarde, although the four baby girls didn't know it at the time."

"Because we were babies," Aamira said, rolling her eyes. "I know I was born blind. We've talked about this before."

"Yes, the fact that you were born blind, but not about the holy magic used to heal you, and how it now is causing all the problems throughout Aarde. Solomon, the protector of Aarde, went to Ishtar and Obatala looking to see if they could find a way to restore the eyesight of the four baby girls. Solomon was unsuccessful, which is why he met with Kaimana and Kainoa. They became aware that Solomon had the power to restore their sight all along providing the four princesses with different eyes. Kaimana and Kainoa divided the chosen bloodlines into four lineages, distinguished by four different colors: Sapphire, Emerald, Hematite Gray, and Turquoise. The Supremes agreed with Solomon that the Black Madonna's would be Aarde's best hope in preventing the eradication of their bloodline on Aarde. Kaimana and Kainoa saw this as a way to save their bloodline, Katunkumene, and Aarde.”

Abioye took a drink of lavender wine. “Sounds coincidental. They only helped because it served their purposes.”

“Indeed. Kaimana and Kainoa knew they could protect the four girls if they ever got separated by attaching signs and events to their eyes that would happen at specific times in their lives. Kaimana and Kainoa told Solomon that they would need protection from the Ukáváál who at one time almost eradicated any trace of their Kemetic blood in the cosmos.”

“The Ancient Kemites were running away from the Ukáváál when they arrived here on Aarde,” Aamira surmised.

“That’s correct,” Adewara said. “The Supremes, Kaimana and Kainoa, traveled inside of Nyathera’s asteroid with all their people. They crashed here and created Sahael. The Orichalcum of the original meteor had magical energy within it that was enhanced by the sun of Aarde. Once the Orichalcum was harvested, Kaimana and Kainoa agreed to a visit by Solomon, who then visited the five flame kepers to transform it into two Sapphires, two Emeralds, two Hematite Gray stones, and two Turquoise stones. Kaimana and Kainoa explained to Solomon the eights stones would be imbued with immense and unlimited power.”

“Wait, so Kaimana and Kainoa tied the fate of Sahael to myself and my three cousins?” Aamira asked.

Adewara tossed a few more nuts in his mouth. “Yes. Kaimana and Kainoa tied the Sapphire stones to the seas of Aarde and life magic. Kaimana and Kainoa tied the Emerald stones with all the life energy on Aarde. Then they tied the Hematite gray stones with spirit energy tied to the clouds in the skies on Aarde. Lastly, they tied the Death energy to the Turquoise stones, and everything buried below the surface of Aarde, which is why, with great concentration, you can manipulate the very stones and dirt around us. All eight of the stones are now connected to the survival of Aarde."

Aamira scratched her eyes. She knew she had been gifted sight by Solomon and the flame keepers as a baby, but now finding out that all the destruction and earthquakes weren't merely tied to some mythical Signs of the Times, but rather Aamira and her cousins' actions? She felt anger suddenly at such an obligation being thrust on them.

"So, a burden was placed on all four Black Madonnas without any thoughts or concerns about any of our desires or wants?" Aamira asked.

"That's correct," Adewara said.

"I didn't sign up for this shit!" Aamira said candidly.

"It matters not what you want or how you feel," Adewara said, equally as candidly. "Those are the cards that you and your cousins have been dealt. A debt was created by your ancestors before you were ever born. It's a sacred debt that must be repaid or Nightfall will surely come to pass. So, get over yourself and your self-pity."

Muscles tensed throughout Aamira's body. She wanted to punch Adewara in the face. Just because what he said may or may not be true, he had no right to so flippantly throw her needs away as if they never mattered.

"You know what, Adewara?" she spat. "You had four men, my sons, who thought the world of you until they discovered what I've known for decades: you're a zealot who sees people as nothing more than tools you can throw away when you're done."

"That's not true," Adewara replied, head shaking.

"It is! I choose to serve. I choose to go to Sahael and save people's lives. I choose! For you, there is no choice. You do things because some damn prophet tells you he saw a vision and you just do what he says. As far as I'm concerned, you're the opposite side of the same coin as Natas. He doesn't believe in free will either."

Adewara stood. "I'm sorry you feel that way."

"I'm not the only one. You hurt my children with your tunnel vision. They all but hate you now because they realize how little you actually care for them."

"I care!" Adewara yelled.

Aamira's head moved back and forth slowly. "You need to think really hard about your actions before you say that. My boys will never follow you with trust again, because they can tell now that you only see them as cogs. You'll need to change that before you can honestly say that you care about any of us."

"I've made sacrifices for the greater good equal to yours and your sons."

"Yes, but the difference is, I care about the fact that you've sacrificed. It pains me to know you have been away from your wife and daughters for years. I feel empathy for you. I share that empathy and in so doing, share a part of myself. I give that part of myself to you freely. It's yours now. You don't give anything of yourself away. I suppose it's the Educator way, but at the end of the day, all it does is leave the rest of us wondering about your motives."

Grabbing the book, Adewara stepped away from the table.

"Adewara," Abioye said, arms raised in a peaceful gesture. "Please stay and finish what you were telling us. Whatever emotions are running high right now, you know we need to know what you've learned. Please continue."

Air rushed into Adewara's lungs as he breathed deeply, looking at his Emperor. He glanced at Aamira.

"Very well. For Sahael. Kaimana and Kainoa decided the signs of the times would be predicated on the four princesses returning to Sahael," Adewara continued, swallowing. "Kaimana and Kainoa told Solomon that if the four princesses ever left Sahael, the signs would be activated, and Aarde would experience death. The signs would then cascade in no particular order."

Aamira took a breath as well, feeling her heart rate slow. "The Invasion of Sahael, and now us yearning for a place to call home, it's happening just as Kaimana and Kainoa said it would. But there had to have been consequences."

"Yes." Adewara sat back down and seemed once again his calm and emotionless self. "Kaimana and Kainoa warned Solomon that the four realms had violated Realm law and the Nairobi laws. Realm law was to be carried out by Naharis's Realm as a means to punish and enforce the strict law created by the Ancient Kemites. To mingle the bloodline's of Alkebulans and Kemettians was forbidden, but to save Aarde, those laws had to be broken for the overall good."

"So, that was the agreement to keep the bloodlines from mingling," Aamira stated.

Opening the book, Adewara began to read. *"In the days before the coming of the Madonnas, Naharis's realm will be responsible for the three realms doling out punishments with extreme prejudice. Naharis's Realm will violate realm law and Nairobi law as well. Kaimana and Kainoa in their anger will cut off their contact with the four realms, leaving them to fend for themselves and call upon the gods in weariness and grief."*

"Due to the realms transgressions, they were forsaken?" Aamira asked.

"So, that must have left Aarde vulnerable," Abioye said.

"Indeed," Adewara continued. "Our order had figured out that Damien took control of Naharis's realm and learned about Nullify's Gate, which revealed the location of the other three realms. Solomon took every precaution, ensuring that the redundancies were in place to prevent the revelation of the locations of the other realms."

"What were those precautions?" Aamira asked.

"No one but Solomon knows," Adewara said. He rubbed his chin. "At least we can find hope in this next passage, which I believe is taking place now because of your attainment of Inkalamu's heart. *The currents have been restored, oh Ishtar, generating life once more in Aarde; especially in Aarde. The restoration of plant life has begun, oh great Obatala, mother of soil, returning to Aarde her fertility. The animals are reproducing once more. It is slow and methodical, as is thy ways, but the beginning is taking shape. These events will continue to happen; the hurricanes, typhoons, and tsunamis; the quakes, tornadoes, and landslides. Everywhere on every continent, thy righteous destruction will continue, oh Ishtar, except for Alkebulan, thy holy jewel. Here thy bloodlines will flourish once more until the world is folded in thy hands, and the son of Ishtar and Obatala be cast out once more.*"

"'Righteous destruction' sounds a bit foreboding," Aamira said.

Adewara opened his mouth to speak, when the sun seemed to dim suddenly. Aamira looked out past the canopy to the crystals overhead, barely visible through the thick mists. They ebbed and flowed with energy, but nowhere near as brightly as they had moments before.

"What's happening?" Abioye asked.

Standing, Adewara stepped out from under the canopy, gazing up at the crystals. "Something is wrong."

"Father!" Lanae shouted as she rushed into the courtyard.

"Lanae! What's wrong, Daughter?"

She rushed over and grabbed her father's arm. "The Laws of Death are being violated."

"Laws of Death?" Aamira asked..

"They have been violated," Lanae said.

"How do you know?" Adewara asked.

Lanae pointed upward toward the crystals. "About an hour ago, Councilman Saulren was communing with the crystal shards when they began to change color. He sent for me, knowing what he was feeling would cascade through the crystals of Inheritance. That is why the sunlight has dimmed. There is something at play that is happening in Aarde; a dark whiteness driving the decisions of witan men right now. That same dark whiteness lurks in the consciousness of Aarde in the form of something that cannot be distinguished. That force hides behind the eyes of these witan men that see blacks as chattel; something to own and control, to be broken down into submission."

"I am aware of this," Adewara replied. He motioned toward Aamira and Abioye. "We have seen it at work in the wider world. This white force hides behind the emptiness of past transgressions, clinging to the trenches of xenophobia and the muck of whiteness. This 'white darkness' as we call it, has convinced the majority of witans to follow Natas into the shadows of consciousness and the depths of despondency by convincing them to eradicate one specific type of people in Aarde. Yet this white darkness cares not for the Black individuals, male or female, even children."

"So much hatred for a group of people, all because they

have Black skin. It never made sense to me." Aamira said. She left the table and looked up at the crystals. The light had dimmed from noonday to evening in an instant. Colors throbbed in dark purple and red.

"Sahael is supposed to stand up and protect all Black people," Abioye said as he stood from the table as well and joined the others in the moist air. "Sahael stands with all Black people in solidarity, whose bodies are theirs to protect. Their sovereignty is theirs to defend, and their freedom is their birthright."

Adewara turned toward Lanae. "What else did Councilman Saulren feel when in communion with the crystals? There must have been more if it is affecting Inheritance in this way."

"There was more," she replied. "Sahael, Horn, Egyptus and Alkebulan are the countries that will bring life into existence on Aarde. It's not a place for witan men with darkness behind their eyes and in their hearts. Saulren told me that he felt Aarde shudder as dead bodies all over the world are being dug up by the ten Ennead Legions."

A look of shock appeared on Adewara's face.

Aamira didn't quite understand Adewara's apparent surprise. "As much as I can remember, the Ennead have always assumed the responsibility of bringing dead bodies back to Naharis Realm."

"That's incorrect," Adewara said. "That responsibility once belonged to the Nelioans, who were overrun by Lord Lieutenant Damien and his Nethanite army." He paused and took a breath. "The Hosts are coming."

"What are the Hosts?" Abioye asked.

Rubbing his neck, Adewara's eyes moved back and forth in their sockets rapidly. "The Hosts are lifeless nomad spirits consumed with nothing but hate and white darkness; all they know is the concept of death. Our bodies and bloodlines are protected by the four ancient laws, the six sacred laws, and the nine divine laws, all within Sahael. These laws may have all been violated, such violations could allow someone the ability to control and manage death."

"I don't understand," Aamira admitted, wiping moisture from her forehead. "How could anyone control death? It's death. You simply pass through it. Death isn't an entity. I've read enough texts over the past 30 years to know that much."

"But imagine," Adewara said, stepping closer to Aamira, "if spirits passing through death became wayward and trapped because of their own choices while in life. The misery they caused affects their ability to move past this plane of existence. They become wanderers, not even remembering who they were in life. If anyone could ever control these spirits, they would have an army that could possess the bodies of the dead and raise a force never felt on Aarde before. Whoever achieved that power would be unchecked and unchallenged, not having to answer to any of the powerful Nations in Aarde."

"Has anyone been able to achieve the ability to control death?" Aamira asked with wide eyes. "How can one gain power over death and then control death?

"We don't know," Lanae said. "But if the Ennead are gathering bodies and even digging them up from their graves, it seems someone believes they can do it."

"Is there a way we can find out?" Abioye asked.

"There is a way," Adewara said. "By traveling to N'eropoili."

Aamira nodded in understanding. "N'eropoili, the island nation where the city of Nycea is."

"The Council of Nycea is where Natas began to take

control," Abioye said, anger evident on his face."

"Yes," Adewara confirmed. "It is the homeland of the Natasians and from where the Ennead are concentrated and launch all their endeavors due to being under Natas's control. If we can make it there, we could learn what is happening and perhaps do something to stop it. At the very least, we can find out who believes they can control the Host, and whether or not they're correct."

Another journey. Aamira wanted nothing to do with it. She wanted to rest, maybe see her boys get married and start families of their own, not travel a thousand miles to the center of an enemy completely enthralled to Natas. How would they even get there? They would need to sail again with Abdul, which would make them a target as they drew closer to N'eropoili. This would be a suicide mission.

"How do you expect us to get there?" Aamira asked. "You're talking about us walking into the center of Ennead power. They would see us coming from a hundred miles away. I may be an impressive fighter, as are my sons, but we wouldn't last ten minutes against an army like that. Even if we took all the warriors from Inheritance, we'd still be crushed."

Adewara shook his head. "Having an army will do us no good. We need to travel with as few people as possible. No more than four. Our advantage would be in subtlety. This is a mission for spies, not warriors." He looked at Abioye. "Your skills will be needed, my Emperor. You were the best spy in IFF, besides me of course."

"What about my sons?" Abioye asked.

"No. They are incredible fighters but not built for this type of work. I would advise just the four of us. Lanae has been well trained since childhood."

"What about me?" Aamira questioned. "I'm a fighter just like my boys."

"We'll need your skill and prowess with a blade, Aamira," Adewara replied.

Aamira shrugged. "Alright, but that still doesn't solve how we get to N'eropoili without being captured on the ocean."

"The Nibiru tunnels," Lanae said.

"Very good idea," Adewara said, pride evident in his voice.

"What are Nibiru Tunnels?" Abioye asked. "Do they lead back to the wall?"

Adewara shook his head. "No, and yes. The tunnels were carved thousands of years ago as merchant highways underground. Now they are all but abandoned. You've been in them before, you just didn't know it."

A memory of underground pathways flashed in Aamira's mind. "When we entered Neros's Realm all those years ago. We used a tunnel system that had glowing crystals embedded in the walls, just like what you have here in Inheritance."

"Exactly," Adewara smiled.

"Do we know how long it will take us to get to N'eropoili?" Abioye asked.

"Several months," Adewara answered. "We'll need to travel on foot."

"What about supplies?" Aamira asked. If they were going to travel for several months underground, food would become an issue.

"There are creatures in the tunnels that are edible," Lanae replied. "My sisters and I have spent days exploring before, living off the water from springs and eating either mushrooms or large grubs. Fire won't be an option, but you get used to eating the grubs raw."

Raw grubs. Worms and maggots. Mushrooms living off the glow from the crystals. That is all Aamira would be eating for the next few months. The thought made her hungry for some pork and a stiff wine.

Adewara turned and walked back toward the table, grabbing his large book. "I will tell the council about our plan. They will be concerned about the dimming of the crystals. We will go to N'eropoili, solve this problem, and then we can return to Inheritance. After that we can move our people to Timbuktu using the ships in the Nibiru lake that empties into eastern Aarde and make our way to Sahael."

"Will the crystals stay dim like this?" Aamira asked.

"I don't think so," Lanae answered. "Normally when we have a disturbance like this, the flow of energy reasserts itself in a matter of days. Hopefully, that will be the case this time as well."

"We leave at first light," Adewara said as he walked out of the courtyard.

When the morning approached, all preparations had been made by Adewara and Lanae for the four spies to travel smoothly through the Nibiru tunnels. An access point existed on the northern side of the cave system where the council, Adewara's other daughters, and Yekú, Yemí, Yomí and Yinká all waited to say their goodbyes. The tunnel entrance was a circular doorway about twenty feet tall with different runes carved into the rock around it.

The council members had chanted and sang a song in a language Aamira did not recognize, and the door had slid open like a stone rolling away from a tomb. After a brief farewell, the four of them entered the tunnels and started walking.

The tunnel walls were smooth, with glowing crystals clustered at intervals on the walls. Aamira noticed that the crystals were similar to the ones all around Inheritance which somehow captured the light of day and would change color and dim at dusk. Water would drip at times off in the dark, but other than the sound of their footfalls, silence reigned. It was going to be a very long few months.

The four of them traveled for six days until they reached a four-way split in the Nibiru tunnels. They turned toward the right and continued in that direction for weeks until they came to another split. They took the left and kept going. Much like her father, Lanae didn't talk much unless someone asked her a question. When they would set up camp for the night, Aamira would ask Lanae about life in Inheritance, her relationship with her sisters, even their mother, but Lanae's answers were always short and pointed, with few details. She was an Educator through and through.

Every day they would look for water and dig up worms and large beetle larvae to eat. Sometimes the grubs were eight inches long. While not flavorful, after a few weeks Aamira grew to tolerate their texture.

After two months, one afternoon Aamira noticed a distinct change in the scent of the air.

"It smells like sewage," she said, holding her hand over her nose.

A strange excitement lit up Adewara's face. "We're close! Look for side tunnels and collapsed access points. If my cartography is correct, we are only a few miles from the city of Nith."

After searching for several hours, Abioye found septic water running from a section of collapsed side tunnel. They followed the branch until it hooked up to a sewer tunnel leading toward the surface. Shafts of light shot through the darkness and Aamira realized she was looking at sewer covers above. She could hear the faint sounds of a city.

"Let's see where we are," Abioye said as he pushed on one of the sewer covers to get a better look at the city. "There is an alley above us. This will be the best place to exit."

They climbed from the tunnel between two buildings made of brick and mortar. The breeze smelled of bread and grilled meats, a welcome scent from the sewer and months of stifled tunnel air. The feeling of the sun on Aamira's skin brought a smile to her face.

"Where do we go from here?" Abioye asked.

"Let's get our bearings," Adewara replied.

"And then some food," Aamira whispered.

They walked stealthily to the mouth of the alley, crouching behind a cluster of wooden barrels. Two-and-three-storied buildings, most of which were old and decaying, made up what they could see of the city. The streets were made of mud with no paving to speak of. People shambled along with an almost aimless gait. At first Aamira thought they were witans, but soon realized they were Black Albinos. Thousands of Black Albinos roamed the streets humming a tune in unison.

"I thought all of the Black Albinos were dead, save only a few," Abioye said.

"No," Adewara whispered. "Lord Commander Natas

cursed all Black Albinos after the fall of Sahael with the Blight; a discriminatory policy authorizing witans the right to hunt, torment, and kill any Black Albino."

"What are they humming?" Aamira asked, uncomfortable tingles running up her back in response to the sound.

"Look at their eyes," Adewara pointed. "They are dull and lifeless. These people have been treated like cattle and now act as little more than cattle. It has been rumored for decades that the city of Nith was turned into a hunting preserve, for lack of a better term, and it looks like that is the truth. Narsans hunt Black Albinos for their magical healing abilities and other ailments their bodies are used for, all myths of course."

Shouting drew their attention down the street where an albino in black robes and golden chains over his shoulders stood on a platform and shouted at the people. He looked like the preachers Aamira would see traveling the plantations in her youth.

"Once the scattering of all of the Blacks is complete, all witans will be able to travel freely all over Aarde as our dominance spreads," The Preacher yelled. "Once the twelve bloodlines are destroyed, then we will have our salvation, as the hosts look to take over and consume bodies to create an army that will cover Aarde in darkness for all of eternity," The preacher said.

"This is crazy!" Aamira said. "He's preaching against his own people. Even though they're of the albino bloodline; they're still Black!"

"Nightfall will help wipe out all of Sahael so that all witans can enslave Alkebulan!" The preacher cried. People in the crowd cheered. "We are of the witan bloodline, despite our black features! This is why we are less than our witan brothers! We deserve our punishments!"

Aamira spat on the ground. "I can't listen to any more of

this garbage."

"What is our path, Father?" Lanae asked.

Adewara glanced up and down the street, pointing to the north. "Put on your cloaks and hoods. We head toward the center of the island where the Narsan have their fortresses near the capital. When we're in the open, we'll need to walk slowly so we don't draw attention to ourselves.

By the afternoon, the four spies had travelled inland. The island of N'eropoili was covered in lush green grass that blew back and forth in the warm winds coming from the ocean. Aamira and the others hid in the meadows as they traveled, occasionally coming across the carcasses of rhinos, hippos, and Ogres on their way to Nycea. Several times they found entire herds of animals slaughtered, rotting in the sun beside the bodies of Black Albinos. Flies began to fill the air all around the closer they drew to Nycea. The stench was too much to bear.

"Something is wrong here," Aamira said as she stepped over a bloated antelope corpse with arcane runes carved into the hide.

"This is a dark place," Adewara breathed. "If you ever wondered what the Aarde of Natas would look like, this is your template."

As the day progressed, things worsened. Dark clouds formed, the air became stifling and dense, flies roamed in swarms of sentient gray fog. They could now see the outlines of buildings in the distance; the city of Nycea. People could now be seen running through the grasslands on dirt roads, some of them chasing animals and screaming savage cries. Aamira caught a glimpse of one through the grass as the man smashed the head of a pig with a rock. He was witan, bald-headed, wearing only a loincloth. Ash covered his body like gray paint. The man had black eyes and red irises with fangs for teeth. He laughed as he slaughtered the squealing animal.

"What are these people?" Aamira asked, voice barely above a whisper.

"The Nemods," Adewara answered, crouched beside her in the grass. "They are wild men, lost to civilization for centuries. It is prophesied they will feed on the Black Albinos as soon as Nightfall comes upon Aarde."

Abioye covered his mouth, face a mask of disgust. "That is not a man. He's practically naked and covered in ash."

"The Nemods are also castrated, according to the few documents I've read about them," Lanae added. "The women have their upper and lower extremities covered in ash as well, with both of their breasts cut off. They are bald, ensuring they all look identical to the men. The Nemods are practically mindless and have been experimented on multiple times for reasons beyond their understanding."

"What type of experimentation?" Aamira asked.

Lanae shrugged.

Adewara moved backwards, away from the bald madman. "Let's move toward Nycea. We've come a long way. If someone is controlling the Host, we need to find out and return to Inheritance before all is lost."

Roads began to crisscross the meadows, some leading toward the city, others toward individual fortresses. On the outskirts of the Nycea, they came upon an estate with iron gates and a large manor house that reminded Aamira of her youth on the plantation. The house seemed to have been abandoned. Statues of a man holding a globe stood 15 feet tall at the gate entrance where rusted metal hung crooked from the stone pillars.

"Is that a statue of Natas?" Abioye asked.

"No," Adewara replied. "The statue has an afro, not long dreadlocks like Natas. These are statues of Damien, the son of Natas. He runs these lands and is treated like the savior of all Aarde."

"Is this Damien's estate then?" Aamira queried.

"No," Adewara answered again, motioning for the others to follow him back into the tall grass. "Damien's estate will be opulent and kept in perfect order for his return. If we find it, that would be the first place we should look for documentation or whisperings of anything regarding the Hosts."

Night fell. They passed several other estates in the dying light of day before finding a massive complex with a twenty-foot-tall stone wall surrounding it. Carvings of Natas and Damien covered the towering barrier. Fires burned in iron bowls at the top of the wall, with Nemod men and women patrolling the perimeter.

"This has got to be Damien's estate," Abioye said. "All the surrounding roads lead toward this manor or back toward the city."

"I think you're right," Adewara agreed.

Quietly, the four of them scaled the walls in between patrols and dropped into the inner sanctuary. The manor house was indeed opulent, with candles burning throughout as if a party were about to be thrown. Hedges were trimmed in the likeness of humans and beasts, with more statues of Damien everywhere Aamira looked. A few Narsan guards wandered here and there with spears, but other than that, the night was quiet.

Aamira, Abioye, Adewara, and Lanae entered the house stealthily. It was evident that Dameon had not been there for a significant amount of time. Dust settled on every surface, save the floors, which were polished and bright. Everything else on the main level of the manor was covered in cobwebs.

"Why are there no guards inside the house?" Aamira asked as she peered out a window toward a group of Narsans sitting around a firepit eating what looked like roasted chicken. Her stomach growled.

"Not even Natas himself would expect an enemy to be stupid enough to infiltrate this island," Adewara said as he rifled through a pile of documents on a table. "The Nemods are enough of a deterrent."

Abioye stood behind a pillar, constantly looking into the dark night for movement from the enemy. "And what if we're discovered, or an alarm is sounded?"

"I assume the Nemods would attack in force, trying to rape and eat us," Lanae said with a matter-of-fact tone Aamira didn't appreciate.

"Then let's move fast!" Abioye urged.

Adewara continued his search upstairs where fewer candles had been lit. They approached the large oak door with a carving of Damien on the front.

"This has to be his personal chambers," the Educator breathed. "Even if we learn nothing about the Host, we may very well discover information that could alter the coming war. Be vigilant."

The door creaked as they entered. No candles were lit in here, so Aamira activated her dark vision and manifested a small glowing blade to help them navigate the room. The space was very large, with a bed twenty feet square anchoring the northern end.

"There's parchment on the table over here," Lanae said. "Bring the light."

Several parchments of paper lay on Damien's desk with the twelve symbols of the ancient bloodline on them.

"Look here," Adewara said, holding up a map with glowing lines that shifted as he moved the paper. "Damien is in possession of Nephrophida's interactive map that reveals the locations of the sacred tribes in western Aarde. Fascinating."

"This document has the sigils of the eye of providence, the red templar cross, and the square and compass," Lanae informed. "It's coded, but the sigils are the key to unlocking it."

Adewara and Lanae sat for the next half hour deciphering the coded message.

"This is about the Trinity," Adewara said. "This information shows that Damien found the bloodlines of western Aarde and converted them after manipulating the Rysallians and merging their bloodlines. It appears Damien was in the process of looking for sacred bloodlines."

"The trinity isn't like the other bloodlines," Lanae said. "The trinity is formidable; they're considered the enlightened ones by Damien, who lived in Eastern Aarde and found a way into Western Aarde. The Trinity never chose to follow Lord Commander Natas. The minds of the Trinity were poisoned by white darkness, so the Trinity, absent free will, were forced to follow Lord Natas. It forced the Trinity to defy the orders of Ishtar and Obatala. This is why Obatala sent the chosen bloodlines to Aarde to protect Sahael, Egyptus, and Horn, ensuring the Black Alkebulans, all would be safe."

Lanae and Adewara continued looking through Damien's archive and saw that Damien had detailed journals of the war in Katunkumene. They learned that Damien had been infected with the white darkness but hadn't led on or revealed to anyone that he played a part in the war. It was Damien's, and his father's, idea that everyone could be saved if he created a plan promising that all of Ishtar and Obatala's children could return to Katunkumene. Damien had visited the realms of outer darkness afterward and was exposed to the white darkness as Nyathera's asteroid passed above Katunkumene.

"All this time Damien wanted to see Katunkumene destroyed," Adewara whispered. "He was sent to the realms of darkness after the Supremes, Kaimana and Kainoa, arrived, making him highly bitter."

"According to Damien's journal, the judges Nineveh, Anubis, and Lord Commander Natas were cast out after Natas's coup attempt in Katunkumene," Lanae said.

"Is there anything in there regarding the Hosts?" Aamira asked.

Adewara nodded slowly. "The last entry mentions Damien's intent to control the Hosts. It is brief but claims he and his father have found a way to bind the spirits of the angry wanderers to the bodies of the dead."

"Does it mention anything else?" Abioye questioned. "Any way to stop him, or by what means they're planning to awaken the hosts in these bodies?"

Lanae looked at her father and let out a slow breath. "The Ukáváál."

Damn it, Aamira thought. The Ukáváál were a whispered enemy, zombies of dead flesh, arcane science, and machine, who destroyed Kolob and the most powerful race of people in the cosmos. They infected everything they touched, killing, eating, or converting their victims, always expanding their army. Adewara had taught her boys about them in their youth back in Karnak, mentioning that Ukáváál existed on Aarde somewhere, but few people knew about that fact. Where the creatures were Aamira could only guess, but if the Ukáváál were involved in Damien's plan to harness the evil power of the Hosts, all of Aarde could fall in a single generation. There would be no more slavery, no more pain and suffering, because everyone would be dead; consumed by a force too destructive to comprehend.

"We need to leave," Abioye said. "Do we want to go into the city under cover of night and see if we can learn anything else?"

"I think we have enough," Adewara replied. He stuffed several volumes of Damien's journal in his pack. "I'm taking these with us. There is more here we can learn from. Let's head straight back to Nith and the tunnel entrance. I think---"

A loud howling made Aamira jump in surprise. She ran to the window.

"What is it?" Abioye asked. "What's that sound?"

Aamira looked down on hundreds of bald Nemods surrounding the house. They carried torches and axes, screaming into the night as one terrifying voice. Their naked bodies shook with fury.

"They know we're here!" she shouted, turning back to the others.

Crashing sounds suddenly echoed from downstairs as windows shattered.

"They're coming!"

"What do we do?" Lanae asked as she moved closer to her father.

Aamira looked outside one more time as the crowd of savage murderers rushed the house like a flock of insane birds.

"We fight," she said, forming blades in each hand. "We fight, or we die."

For a moment she contemplated saying the words that were truly in her mind: *We fight AND we die*, but she knew such truth would not serve them.

[To be concluded in Volume 2 Book 5]

OUT NOW:

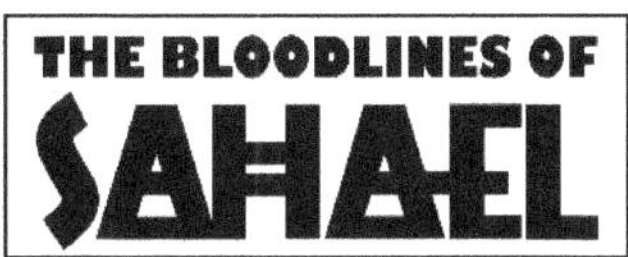

VOLUME TWO

BOOK FIVE

THE YORUBA OF SAHAEL

BY

DWAYNE ANTHONY MADRY

www.ingramcontent.com/pod-product-compliance
Lightning Source LLC
Chambersburg PA
CBHW071431300726
48976CB00004B/1296